CAPTAIN JAMES KIRK: Absolute master of the largest and most modern vessel in the Starfleet service, *USS Enterprise*, and of the manifold talents of the 430 highly trained crewmen; his decisions alone can affect the future course of civilisation throughout the universe.

SCIENCE OFFICER SPOCK: First Officer of the *Enterprise* and, it is said, best First Officer in the whole fleet; his knowledge of computers is total and his mental abilities indispensable. Half Vulcan, half human by birth, Spock is logical to the exclusion of all emotion – except curiosity!

DR. BONES McCOY: Senior Ship's Surgeon and expert in space psychology, McCoy at times appears to be the traditional 'witch doctor' of space as he combats the deadliest and virulent of maladies - whether physical or mental – from all manner of worlds and species with baffling ease!

ADAPTED BY
James Blish

Star Trek 9

CORGI BOOKS
A DIVISION OF TRANSWORLD PUBLISHERS LTD

To Maire Steele

STAR TREK 9
A CORGI BOOK 0 552 09476 5

First publication in Great Britain

PRINTING HISTORY
Corgi edition published 1974

Copyright © 1973 by Bantam Books, Inc.
and Paramount Pictures Corporation

Corgi Books are published by Transworld Publishers Ltd.,
Cavendish House, 57-59 Uxbridge Road,
Ealing, London W.5
Made and printed in Great Britain by
Hunt Barnard Printing Ltd, Aylesbury, Bucks.

Contents

PREFACE

There is a lot of mail to be caught up on this time, and some news. However, a book is not a newspaper, so some of the news may be contradicted by later events, and certainly stale, by the time you read this.

First of all, there was a Star Trek convention in New York last January. The organizer expected perhaps five hundred people. He got nearly four thousand—which makes this gathering, incidentally, the largest science-fiction convention in history. It was covered in some depth by *TV Guide* and by several major newspapers.

Gene Roddenberry was there, and told both the audience and the press that he hoped for a return of the series. Though quotations of what he actually said make it clear that this was no more than a wish we all share, my mail shows that it created more solid anticipation than it should have.

If you would like to add your voice to those urging NBC to choose in favor of Star Trek, write to: Bettye K. Hoffmann, Manager, NBC Corporate Information, National Broadcasting Company, 30 Rockefeller Plaza, New York, N. Y. 10020. Writing to *me* about it does no good at all; I am only a writer with no influence whatsoever upon NBC except for the known popularity of these books.

I've said several times in the past that though I read all your letters and value them, there are just too many of them for me to answer. There's been no falling off in their numbers since then. Yet not only do I still get requests for personal replies, but many of them enclose American return postage. Even were I able to answer—and I repeat, with apologies, that I just can't

—U.S. stamps are just as useless in England as British stamps would be in the states. Save your money!

From ST 6 on, I'm greatly indebted to Muriel Lawrence, who began by doing a staggering amount of typing for me, and went on from there to take so much interest in *Star Trek* itself that her analyses, suggestions, and counsel have made the adaptations much better than they used to be. And just possibly it may be worth adding, for those among you who believe or fear that anybody over thirty can't possibly understand what inspires people under that age, that we were both of us well past it before *Star Trek* had even been conceived. Idealism lasts, if you love it; and these books would have been impossible without it, just like the show itself.

Be of good cheer. We're not alone, no matter how often we may think we are.

JAMES BLISH

RETURN TO TOMORROW

(Gene Roddenberry and John T. Dugan)

The readings were coming from a star system directly ahead of the *Enterprise*. And havoc is what they were causing. The Starship's distress relays had been activated. All its communication channels had been affected. A direction to follow had even been specified, but no clear signal had been received. Yet one fact was clear: someone or something was trying to attract the Enterprise's attention. Who? Or what? Those were the questions.

Over at Spock's station, Kirk said, "Well?"

"I don't know, Captain."

Despite his exasperation, Kirk smiled. "I never heard you use those words before, Mr. Spock."

"Not even a Vulcan can know the unknown, sir," Spock said stiffly. "We're hundreds of light years past where any Earth ship has ever explored."

"Planet dead ahead, Captain!" Sulu called. "Becoming visual."

The screen showed what appeared to be a very dead planet: scarred, shrunken, a drifting cadaver of a world.

Uhura turned from her board. "That planet is the source of whatever it is we have been receiving, sir."

Spock, his head bent to his hooded viewer, announced, "Class M planet, sir. Oblate spheroid, ratio 1 to 296. Mean density 5.53. Mass .9." He paused. "Close resemblance to Earth conditions with two very important differences. It's much older than Earth. And about half a million years ago its atmosphere was

1

totally ripped away by some cataclysm. Sensors detect no life of any kind."

Without warning the bridge was suddenly filled by the sound of a voice, resonant, its rich deepness profoundly impressive. *"Captain Kirk,"* it said, *"all your questions will be answered in time."*

The bridge people stared at the screen. Kirk, turning to Uhura, said, "Are your hailing frequencies freed yet, Lieutenant?"

"No, sir."

They had sped past the planet now. Eyes on the screen, Kirk said, "Maintain present course, Mr. Sulu."

The deep voice spoke again. *"I am Sargon. It is the energy of my thoughts which has touched your instruments and directed you here."*

"Then, can you hear me?" Kirk asked. "Who are you, Sargon?"

"Please assume a standard orbit around our planet, Captain."

"Are you making a request or demand?" Kirk said.

"The choice is yours. I read what is in your mind: words are unnecessary."

"If you can read my mind, you must know I am wondering just who and what you are. The planet we've just passed is dead; there is no possibility of life there as we understand life."

"And I," said the voice, *"am as dead as my planet. Does that frighten you, Captain? If it does, you will let what is left of me perish."* An awesome solemnity had entered the voice. *"Then, all of you, my children—all of mankind will . . ."*

The voice faded as the Starship moved out of the planet's range. Sulu, turning to Kirk, said, "Do we go on, sir—or do I turn the ship back?"

Kirk could feel all eyes centered on him. Then Spock spoke from his station. "There's only one possible explanation, sir. Pure thought . . . the emanations of a fantastically powerful mind."

Kirk paced the distance from his chair to the main viewing screen. "Whatever it is, we're beyond its range."

"And out of danger," Spock said dryly.

"You don't recommend going back?"

"If a mind of that proportion should want to harm us, sir, we could never hope to cope with it."

"It called me—us 'my children,'" Kirk said. "What could that mean?"

"Again, sir—I don't know."

Kirk sank down in his command chair, frowning. Then his brow cleared. "All right," he said. "Take us back, Mr. Sulu. Standard orbit around the planet."

The dead world gradually reappeared on the screen, its color the hue of dead ash. Sulu said, "Entering standard orbit, Captain."

Kirk nodded, eyes on the screen. Then he hit the button of his command recorder, dictating. "Since exploration and contact with alien intelligence is our primary mission, I have decided to risk the dangers potential in our current situation—and resume contact with this strange planet. Log entry out." Snapping off the recorder, he spoke to Uhura. "How long before Starfleet receives that?"

"Over three weeks at this distance, sir. A month and a half before we receive their answer."

Kirk left his chair to cross to Spock's station. The Vulcan was swiftly manipulating dials.

"Got something?" Kirk said.

"Sensors registering some form of energy, sir . . . deep *inside* the planet."

Sargon's voice came once more. "*Your probes have touched me, Mr. Spock.*"

Spock looked up at Kirk. "I read energy only, sir. No life form."

Then again Sargon spoke. "*I have locked your transporter device on my coordinates. Please come to us. Rescue us from oblivion.*"

Spock, imperturbable, lifted his head from his viewer's mound. "It came from deep under the planet surface, Captain . . . from under at least a hundred miles of solid rock."

Kirk began, "We can't beam—"

Sargon addressed the half-spoken thought in his

3

mind. *"I will make it possible for your transporter to beam you that deep beneath the surface. Have no fear."*

Spock, concentrating on his viewer, said, "I read a chamber beneath the surface, sir. Oxygen-nitrogen suitable for human life support."

Kirk gave himself a long moment. Then he spoke to Uhura. "Lieutenant, have Dr. McCoy report to the Transporter Room in ten minutes with standard landing-party equipment."

"Aye, sir."

"Captain," Spock said, "I am most curious to inspect whatever it is that has survived half a million years—this entity which has outlived its cataclysmic experience."

Kirk laid a hand on his shoulder. "And I'd like my Science Officer with me on something as unusual as this. But it's so full of unknowns, we can't risk the absence of both of us from the ship."

The bridge was instantly plunged into total darkness. All panel hum stilled. Sulu hit a switch. "Power's gone, sir! *Totally* gone!"

There had been no menace in the deep voice. A tone of pleading, yes—but no menace. Kirk frowned, pondering. Then he said, "On the other hand, Mr. Spock, perhaps this 'Sargon' wants you to come along with me."

Lights flashed back on. Panels hummed again. Sulu, checking his board, cried, "All normal, sir! No damage at all."

"Well," Kirk said. "Then that's that. Mr. Spock, you'll transport down with us." As he strode to the elevator, he turned to add, "Mr. Sulu, you have the con."

A young woman, dark and slim, had followed McCoy into the Transporter Room. Kirk recognized her —Lieutenant Commander Anne Mulhall, astrobiologist. His eyes took in the figure, the startling sapphire of the eyes under the raven-black hair. He hadn't remembered her as so attractive. She lowered her eyes, checking her equipment, two security guards beside her. Nor did she look up as McCoy said tartly, "Jim, why no briefing on this? I'd like at least to know—"

Kirk interrupted. "Easy, Bones. If you know 'something is down there,' you know as much as we do. The rest is only guesses."

Scott, over at the Transporter console, spoke. "I don't like it, Captain. Your coordinates preset by an alien of some unknown variety. You could materialize inside solid rock."

"Inside solid rock!" McCoy shouted.

Spock, moving in beside Scott, said, "Unlikely, Doctor. The coordinates correspond to a chamber that sensor readings detected on the bridge."

"It is my feeling," Kirk said, "that they or it could destroy us standing right here if it wanted to, Mr. Scott."

Anne spoke for the first time. "'They' or 'it'?" she said.

Kirk looked at her. "Lieutenant Commander, may I ask what you're doing here in this room?"

"I was ordered to report for landing-party duty, sir."

"By whom?"

"I . . ." She smiled. "It's strange, sir. I'm not sure."

There was a moment's pause. Then, flushing, she added, "I do not lie, Captain. I *did* receive an order to report here."

Spock intervened. "I'm sure she did, Captain. Just as you received an order to take me along."

Kirk nodded; and McCoy said, "Let's get back to this solid-rock business. How much rock are we going through?"

Spock answered. "Exactly one hundred, twelve point three seven miles below the surface, Doctor."

"Miles?" McCoy echoed blankly. "Jim, he's joking!"

But Kirk was assigning Transporter positions to the party. They were taking their places when the console lights abruptly flashed on and Sargon's voice said, *"Please stand ready. I will operate the controls."*

5

Kirk spoke in reaction to the shock in McCoy's face. "If you'd prefer to stay behind, Bones . . ."

McCoy eyed him. "No—no, if I'd be useful, and I may have to be, that is, as long as you're beaming down, Jim . . ." He shrugged. "I might as well have a medical look at whatever this is."

Kirk joined them on the platform. "Energize!" he called to Scott.

The dematerializing shimmer broke them into glittering fragments—all of them except the two security guards. They were left standing, unaffected, on the platform, their faces astounded. Scott stared at them, his face drawing into lines of worry.

The selected group materialized in a metallic vault, some sort of antechamber, its luminescent walls diffusing a softly radiant glow. Spock was the first to realize the absence of the security guards.

Kirk nodded at his comment. "Somebody down here doesn't like them," he said. He opened his communicator. "Kirk here, Scotty."

"Can you read me, Captain?"

"I shouldn't be able to, not from this deep inside the planet. Perhaps that's been arranged for us, too. Is the security team up there?"

"They're fine, Captain. They just didn't dematerialize. I don't like it, sir."

"No problems here yet. Maintain alert. Captain out."

Anne and Spock had been circling the vault with their tricorders. The girl said, "Atmosphere report, Captain. A fraction richer in oxygen than usual for us, but otherwise normal."

Spock had applied his tricorder to a wall. "This vault was fabricated about a half-million years ago. About the same time that the planet surface was destroyed."

"Walls' composition?"

"A substance or alloy quite unknown to me, sir. Much stronger and harder than anything I ever measured."

"All readings go off the scale, sir," Anne said.

6

"The air's fresh," McCoy said, sniffing. "Must be re-circulated somehow."

"For us? Or does 'it' need fresh air?"

As if in reply, the fourth wall of the vault slid back. They recoiled. Ahead of them was a vast room. It was starkly bare, empty except for a large slab of veinless white stone, supported by four plain standards of the same immaculate stone. On it stood a big translucent globe, brilliantly lit from within. The group followed Kirk into the room; but as Spock stepped forward to take a tricorder reading of the globe, he was halted by the sound of Sargon's voice, still deep but no longer resonant.

"Welcome," said the globe. *"I am Sargon."*

Once more Spock focused his tricorder. "Sargon, would you mind if I—?"

"You may use your tricorder, Mr. Spock. Your readings will show energy but no substance. Sealed in this receptacle is the essence of my mind."

Spock took his readings. Then he backed up to Kirk so that he, too, could see them. Kirk gave a low whistle of amazement. "Impossible, Spock! A being of pure energy without matter or form!"

McCoy addressed the globe. "But you once had a body of some type?"

"Although our minds were infinitely greater, my body was much as yours, my children."

Kirk spoke slowly. "That is the second time you have called us your 'children'."

"Because it is probable you are our descendants, Captain. Six thousand centuries ago our vessels were colonizing this galaxy just as your own Starships are now exploring it. As you leave your seed on distant planets, so we left our seed behind us."

Anne protested: "Our studies indicate that our planet Earth evolved independently." But Spock, his face unusually preoccupied, said, "That would explain many enigmas in Vulcan pre-history."

"There is no certainty. It was so long ago that the records of our travels were lost in the catastrophe we loosed upon ourselves."

7

Kirk said, "A war?"

"*A struggle for goal that unleashed a power you cannot even comprehend.*"

"Then perhaps your intelligence was deficient, Sargon." Kirk stepped toward the globe. "We faced a crisis like that at the beginning of the Nuclear Age. But we found the wisdom not to destroy ourselves."

"*We survived our primitive Nuclear Era, my son. But there comes to all races an ultimate crisis which you have yet to face.*"

"I should like to understand," Kirk said. "I do not."

"*The mind of man can become so powerful that he forgets he is man. He confuses himself with God.*"

Kirk's mind was awhirl. Was this being speaking of the Lucifer sin? Abruptly, he felt a completed trust of Sargon. He moved to the globe with the confidence of a child to a parent. "You said you needed help. What is it you wish?"

A strange thrilling sound echoed through the room. In the globe, light fluctuated, growing brighter and brighter. Then a flare broke from it. It transfixed Kirk, holding him immobile. At the same instant light in the globe dimmed to a tiny flicker. It was clear to the others that the essence of what was in the globe had transferred itself to Kirk—and vanished into him.

McCoy started forward, but Spock put out a restraining hand. "Patience, Doctor. Let's wait a moment."

Kirk stood rigid, stiffened, his eyes shut. It seemed centuries to McCoy before they opened, "Jim . . ." he said. "Jim . . ."

Kirk spoke. "I am . . . Sargon."

His voice had deepened. And his bearing had changed, permeated as by the calm, gently austere dignity that had characterized the personality of Sargon.

McCoy yelled, "*Where's our Captain? Where's Jim Kirk?*"

"Here, Bones." The voice of Sargon-Kirk was gentle as a mother soothing a frightened infant. "Your loved

Captain is unharmed. I have taken his body for the moment to demonstrate to you—"

McCoy had drawn his phaser. "No! No, I do not go along with this! Back where you were, Sargon, whatever you are!"

"What do you propose to do with your phaser?" It was the mild voice of Spock. "That's still Jim's body."

McCoy's shoulders slumped. Then he saw that the incorporated Sargon was slowly becoming aware of Kirk's body. It expanded its chest; its head was flung up as the deliciousness of air was inhaled; its arms flexed—and a cry burst from it.

"Lungs . . . lungs savoring breath again! Eyes seeing colors again! A heart pumping arteries surging with young blood!" A hand touched the other one in wonder. "To *feel* again after half a million years!" Kirk's body turned, his own smile on its lips. "Your Captain has an excellent corpus, Doctor! I compliment both of you on the condition in which it has been maintained."

"And your plans for it?" Spock's voice was toneless. "Can you exchange places again when you wish?"

Sargon-Kirk didn't answer. Instead, he moved to the receptacle with its frail glow of light. Pointing to it, he said, "Have no fear. Your Captain is quite unharmed in there." The dim flicker slightly brightened. "See? He hears, he knows, he is aware of all we do and say. But his mind cannot generate the energy to speak from the globe as I did."

Spock, who had been using his tricorder, called "Doctor!" McCoy paled as he saw its readings. "The creature is killing him!" he shouted. "Heartbeat almost double, temperature one hundred and four degrees!"

"Sargon, what is it you want of us?" Spock demanded.

Kirk's eyes studied them silently. Finally Sargon's words came. "There are other receptacles in the next room; they contain two more of us who have survived. You, Anne Mulhall, and you, Mr. Spock—we shall require your bodies for them. We must have your bodies and Captain Kirk's in order to live again."

It had come to all of them that Kirk was no longer Kirk but an individual stronger, wiser, infused with a dominant intelligence beyond the reach of any of them. Waved into the next room, they obediently moved into it. Its shelved walls held many receptacles; but of them all, only two still shone with light. Kirk's deeper voice said, "Yes, only two of us still live. The others are blackened by death but these two still shine —Hanoch and Thalassa." He caressed one of the lighted globes. "Thalassa, my Thalassa, I am pleased you survived with me. Half a million years have been almost too long to wait."

Spock said, "Sargon, when that struggle came that destroyed your planet . . ."

"A few of the best minds were chosen to survive. We built these chambers and preserved our essence here in this fashion." He touched the Thalassa globe with tenderness. "My wife, as you may have guessed. And Hanoch from the other, enemy side in the struggle. By then we had all realized our mistake."

He paused. "We knew the seeds we had planted on other planets had taken root. And we knew you would one day build vessels as we did—that you would come here."

"What was your task in that globe out there?" Spock said.

"To search the heavens with my mind . . . probing, waiting, probing. And finally my mind touched something—your ship bringing you here."

"So you could thieve our bodies from us!" Anne cried.

He looked at her, the centuries of gathered wisdom in his eyes contrasting eerily with the youth of Kirk's face. "To steal your bodies? No, no. You misunderstand, my children. To *borrow* them. We ask you to only lend them to us for a short time."

"To *destroy* them!" cried McCoy. "Just as you're burning that one up right now! Spock, the heartbeat reading is now 262! And the whole metabolic rate is just as high! My medical tricorder—"

10

"I shall return your Captain's body before its limit has been reached, Doctor."

"What is the purpose of this borrowing?" Spock said.

"To build . . ." Suddenly, Sargon-Kirk swayed. Then he straightened. "To build humanoid robots. We must borrow your bodies only long enough to have the use of your hands, your fingers."

Spock turned to the others. "I understand," he said. "They will construct mechanical bodies for themselves and move their minds into them. That accomplished, they will return our bodies to us."

Anne interposed. "We have engineers, technicians. Why can't they build the robot bodies for you?"

"No. Our methods, the skill required, goes far beyond your abilities." He swayed again, staggering, and Spock put out an arm to support him. His breath was coming hard and the Vulcan had to stoop to hear his whisper. "It is . . . time. Help me back to your . . . Captain."

With McCoy at his other side, he stumbled back into the big bare room. Weakly, he waved them aside to stand alone by the receptacle, eyes closed. This time the flare of light flashed from him—and abruptly, the globe was again alive with a pulsating brilliance. The knees of the borrowed body gave way and Anne Mulhall rushed to it, her arms outstretched. They closed around its shoulders and its eyelids fluttered open. "Captain Kirk?" she said tentatively.

The skipper of the *Enterprise* smiled at her, his eyes on her face.

"Jim . . . is it you?" cried McCoy.

Kirk didn't speak, his gaze still deep in the sapphire eyes. Hurriedly, McCoy checked him with his medical tricorder. "Good—good, fine! Metabolic rate back to normal!"

Spock went to him. "Captain, do you remember what happened? Do you remember any part of it?"

"What? Oh. Oh, yes, yes. Sargon borrowed my body." He gestured to the globe. "I was there, floating . . . floating in time and space."

"You take it damned casually!" McCoy said. "However, you don't seem harmed . . . physically at least."

Kirk, wholly himself again, suddenly seemed to realize how matter-of-factly he was accepting his extraordinary experience. "Spock, I remember all now! As Sargon and I exchanged—for an instant we were one. I know him. I know now exactly what he is and what he wants. *And I do not fear him.*"

Anne had withdrawn her embrace. "Captain, I'm afraid I must agree with Dr. McCoy. You could be suffering mental effects from this—a kind of euphoria."

"There's a way to check my conviction about Sargon." He turned to Spock. "I—I hate to ask it, Mr. Spock, knowing as I do what it costs you."

"Vulcan mind-melding?" McCoy said. "Are you willing, Spock?"

Spock took time to answer. Finally, he nodded gravely. Then, with care, he began to ready himself for the ordeal, breathing deeply, massaging chest muscles. Kirk, turning to the globe, said, "Sargon, we—"

"*I understand. I am prepared.*"

It began. The globe's brilliance increased and, with it, the strain on Spock's anguished concentration. His breath grew harsh and his neck muscles taut. Words started to come like those of a man in a dream or a nightmare. ". . . there is a world . . . not physical. The mind reaches . . grows to encompass . . . to understand beyond understanding . . . growing . . . beyond comprehension . . . beyond . . . beyond . . . beyond . . ."

Kirk flashed an alarmed look at McCoy. It had never been so hard. They started forward—but Spock himself was now breaking away from the meld. He drew a deep lungful of breath, shaking, weak, eyes dazed.

"Spock?" Kirk cried.

The voice still held the awe of inexpressible experience. "Captain, I cannot say . . . what I have seen. The—the knowledge . . . the beauty of perfect reason . . . the incredible goodness . . . the unbelievable glory of ageless wisdom . . . the pure goodness of what Sargon is . . ."

Anne was the first to break the silence. "Beauty? Perfect reason? Pure goodness?"

Kirk nodded. "Beyond imagination."

Spock, still shaken, whispered, "It . . . will take me . . . time to absorb all I have learned . . . all I have felt . . ."

"Yes," Kirk said. Instinctively he turned to the receptacle. "Sargon . . ." he said. The word might have been "Father".

"I understand, my son. Go to your vessel. All who are involved must agree to this. After all these centuries, we can wait a few more hours."

McCoy strode to the globe. "And if we decide against you?"

"Then you may go as freely as you came."

Leonard McCoy was out of his depth. He looked from Spock to Kirk, feeling himself to be the alien in a world no longer familiar to him. He had never been so uncertain of himself in his life.

"You are going to *what?*"

Scott had leaned over the Briefing Room table, his face incredulous. Kirk, quite composed, sat beside the grim-jawed McCoy. He smiled at Scott; and his Chief Engineer, Highland blood boiling, cried, "Are they all right in the head, Doctor?"

"No comment," McCoy said.

"It's a simple transference of our minds and theirs, Scotty," Kirk said.

"Nothing to it," McCoy said. "It happens every day."

Kirk ignored him. "I want your approval, Scotty. You'll have to do all the work with them, furnishing all they need to build the android robots. That is, you'll only seem to be working with us—with our bodies. But they'll be inside of them and we will be . . ." The explanation was getting complicated. Kirk flinched under the cold Scottish steel of Scott's eyes. "We'll be . . . in their receptacles," he finished lamely.

He sounded mad to his own ears. Where had fled

that supremely sane self-possession of Sargon's that his body had entertained so briefly? He struggled to recover some shred of it; and McCoy cried, "Where they'll be, Scott, is floating in a ball! Just drifting sweetly in a ball of nothing! Indecent is what it is—indecent!"

Spock spoke. "Once inside their robot forms, Engineer, they will restore our bodies. They can leave this planet and travel back with us. With their massive knowledge, mankind can leap ahead ten thousand years."

"Bones," Kirk said, "they'll show us medical miracles you've never dreamed possible. And engineering advances, Scotty! Vessels this size with engines no larger than a walnut!"

"You're joking," Scott said gruffly.

"No," Spock said. "I myself saw that and more in Sargon's mind. I encountered an infinity of a goodness and knowledge that—that at this moment still staggers me."

"Many a fine man crushes ants underfoot without even knowing it." McCoy's voice shook. "They're giants and we're insects beside them, Jim. They could destroy us without meaning to."

Scott was musing aloud. "A Starship engine the size of a walnut?" He shrugged. "Impossible. But I suppose there's no harm in looking over diagrams on it . . ."

"And all he wants for these miracles is the body of our ship's Captain," McCoy said. "And that of our next in command, too. Coincidence? Anybody want to bet?"

"They have selected us, Bones, as the most compatible bodies."

"And your attitude on that, Dr. Mulhall?" McCoy demanded.

"If we all agree," Anne said steadily, "I am willing to host Thalassa's mind. I am a scientist. The opportunity is an extraordinary one for experimentation and observation."

"Bones, you can stop this right now by voting 'no'.

That's why I called you all here. We'll all be deeply involved. It must be unanimous."

McCoy slammed the table. "Then I still want one question answered! *Why?* Not a list of possible miracles—but an understandable, simple, basic 'why' that doesn't ignore all the possible dangers! Let's not kid ourselves! There's much danger potential in this thing!"

"They used to say, Bones, that if man were meant to fly, he'd have wings. But he *did* fly." Kirk's voice deepened with his earnestness. "In fact, human existence has been a long story of faint-hearted warnings not to push any further, not to learn, not to strive, not to grow. I don't believe we can stop, Bones. Do you want to return to the days when your profession operated with scalpels—and sewed up the patients with catgut?"

He paused, looking at the faces around the table. "Yes, I'm in command. I can order this. I haven't done so. Dr. McCoy is performing his duty. He is right to point out the enormous danger potential in such close contact with intelligence as fantastically advanced as this. *My* point is that the potential for new knowledge is also enormous. Risk is our business. That's what this Starship is all about! It is why we're aboard her!"

He leaned forward in his chair, his eyes searching faces. "You may dissent without prejudice. Do I hear a negative vote?"

There was none. He rose to his feet. "Mr. Scott, stand by to bring the three receptacles aboard."

In Sickbay the three beds had been arranged for Kirk, Spock, and Anne. A shining globe had been placed beside each one. McCoy, Christine Chapel beside him, stood at the body-function panels, his clipboard in hand. He turned to the nurse. "You must know," he said, "that with the transfer, the extreme power of the alien minds will drive heart action dangerously high. All body functions will race at many times normal metabolism. These panels must be monitored most carefully."

The situation had shaken Christine. She made a successful effort to recover her professionalism. "Yes, sir," she said.

McCoy spoke to Kirk. "We're about as ready as we'll ever be."

Kirk turned his head to the globe beside him. "Ready, Sargon."

There came the thrilling sound preceding transfer. The three globes grew active, light building and fluctuating inside them. Then the three flares flashed from them to the bodies lying on the beds. Anne's trembled as Thalassa entered it. Christine moved quickly to check it. Hanoch-Spock sat up, stretching in delight at the feel of a body. Beside each bed the globes' light had dimmed to a faint flicker. McCoy was concentrated on Kirk's body-function panel; and Christine, leaving Thalassa-Anne, moved in to check Hanoch-Spock. To her amazement, he smiled at her, his eyes taking her in with lusty appreciation. Where was the cool, cerebral Spock?

She turned hastily to his body panel. What she read alarmed her. "Metabolic rates are double and rising, Doctor."

Hanoch-Spock spoke. "A delicious woman . . . a delicious sight to awaken to after half a million years."

Disconcerted, Christine said, "Thank you."

But Hanoch-Spock was looking beyond her now to where Thalassa-Anne was sitting up in bed, raven hair about her shoulders, the blue eyes shining as she savored the forgotten feeling of life. "I—I didn't remember what it felt like . . . to breathe—to breathe like this!" She turned. "Sargon? Where's Sargon?"

Sargon-Kirk rose and went to her. "Here . . . in this body, Thalassa." With a becoming dignity, threaded with joy in the awakening of long-forgotten senses, she smiled at him. "The body does not displease me, my husband. It is not unlike that which was your own."

"I am pleased by your pleasure, my love."

She had become aware of her hands. Tentatively, she reached one up to caress his cheek. "After so long," she whispered. "It's been so long, Sargon."

His arms were around her. Christine averted her eyes as their lips met. There was something infinitely touching in this embrace, longed for but deferred for half a million years. They separated and Christine said, "I'm sorry . . . I'm here . . ."

Thalassa-Anne extended a gentle hand. "You are not intruding, my child. As a woman, you know my wondrous gratitude at touching him who is mine again. Do you have a man?"

"No. I—I . . ." Despite herself, Christine found her eyes moving to Spock, forgetting for the moment that it was Hanoch who inhabited him. She flushed. "No, I . . . do not have that need. I have my work." She took a hasty reading of the body-function panel. Had Hanoch-Spock noticed that look?

Thalassa-Anne spoke quietly to Sargon. "How cruel. May I help her, my husband?"

"It would be so easy to give all of them happiness, Thalassa." He shook his head gently. "But we must not interfere in their lives."

More aggressive than the others, Hanoch-Spock was already circling the room, examining its equipment. He turned to find McCoy watching him. "An excellent body, Doctor. It seems I received the best of the three." He extended his arms, flexing Spock's superb biceps. "Strength, hearing, eyesight, all above the human norm. I'm surprised the Vulcans never conquered your race."

"Vulcans prize peace above all, Hanoch."

"Of course. Of course. Just as do we."

But McCoy had seen Thalassa-Anne sink back on her pillow. "Nurse!"

The lovely alien whispered, "A wave of heat suddenly . . . I feel . . ."

Christine caught her as she sagged, drawing in the support of another pillow behind her. McCoy was assisting her when he saw Sargon-Kirk begin to slump. As he supported him to his bed, he said, "Hanoch, you'd better go back to bed, too."

But Spock's metabolism had not yet been affected.

Hanoch said, "Unnecessary at present, Doctor. My Vulcan body is accustomed to higher metabolism."

Christine tore her eyes from him to check Thalassa-Anne's body-function panel. Its readings were alarmingly high. McCoy rushed to the bed at the nurse's call. Then he whirled to the bed that held Sargon-Kirk. "It won't work, Sargon! You've got to get out of them before you kill them!"

The answer came weakly. "We will . . . vacate them . . . until you can administer . . . a metabolic-reduction injection."

"A what?" McCoy demanded.

Hanoch-Spock joined him at the bed, looking down at Kirk's sweaty forehead. "I will prepare the formula, Sargon," he said.

"Hanoch . . . your own condition . . ."

"I can maintain this body for several more hours, Sargon. Do not be anxious."

"Then . . . Thalassa and I . . . will now return to our confinement."

Beside the beds of Kirk and Anne the globes flared with light again. But Hanoch-Spock, still incarnate, gave his dim one a look of repulsion. He turned from Kirk's bed to speak to McCoy. "I shall need help to prepare the formula. Your nurse will assist me, Doctor, in your pharmacology laboratory."

Christine looked at McCoy. He couldn't tell himself that he was confronted by a command decision. That had already been made by Kirk. The decision facing him merely implemented his Captain's wish. He nodded reluctantly—and Christine followed Hanoch-Spock out of Sickbay.

Behind him Kirk and Anne were slowly recovering from the effects of the alien possession. Kirk's eyes at last fluttered open. McCoy had to stoop to hear his whisper.

"Bones . . ."

"It was close, Jim. You and Anne barely got back in time. Unless this formula works, we can't risk another transfer."

In the pharmacology laboratory, two hypos lay on a table. Hanoch-Spock held the third one. He made some adjustment on it, Christine behind him, watching. At last, he spoke. "This formula will reduce heart action and body function to normal. Whenever their bodies are occupied, administer one injection, ten cc.'s every hour."

"I understand," Christine said.

"Code this one for Thalassa. And *this* hypo, code it for me."

"Yes, sir." She affixed the appropriate seals to the hypos.

"Each contains a formula suited to the physical traits of that individual's body."

She pointed to the third hypo. "And that one is for Captain Kirk when Sargon is in his body?

Hanoch-Kirk handed it to her. "Yes. Of course."

Christine had taken the hypo to mark it when she noticed the color of its fluid. She examined it more carefully. Then, troubled, she said, "This hypo doesn't contain the same formula."

Hanoch-Spock smiled. On Spock's usually expressionless face, the smile was extraordinarily charming. "Since I will arrange for you to give the injections, no one else will notice that."

"But—without the correct formula, Captain Kirk will die."

"So he will—and Sargon with him."

Christine, staring, had begun to protest when Hanoch-Spock, reaching out, touched her forehead. Her head swam with dizziness. Then all sensation left her. Entranced where she stood, she could only look at him helplessly.

"Thalassa I can use," he said. "But Sargon must be destroyed. He would oppose me in what I plan. You wish to speak, my dear?"

"Please, I . . . I was . . . I wanted to say something." She passed a hand over her whirling head. "I've . . . forgotten what it was."

He touched her brow again. "You were about to

say you watched me prepare the formula and fill the three hypos with it."

She swayed. "Yes—that was it. I will tell Dr. McCoy that each hypo is properly filled for each patient. You must excuse me. I lost my train of thought for a moment."

"It will not occur again," he said. "You are under my guidance now, child." Looking quickly toward the corridor, he made for the doorway. "And now for Dr. McCoy . . ."

But McCoy had snapped the lab door open. "If you require any further drugs or assistance, Hanoch—"

"I've encountered no difficulties at all, Doctor. I left the formula on your computer if you care to examine it."

In her trance Christine picked up the hypos. She spoke the words implanted in her mind. "I watched them prepared and coded, Doctor. Shall I take them to Sickbay?"

McCoy nodded. As the door closed behind her, Hanoch-Spock smiled. "It's good to be alive again, Doctor. I will find it most difficult when the time comes to surrender this body I so enjoy.

Was it the implication of the last words that disturbed McCoy? Or was it the shock of the excessively charming smile on Spock's face? He didn't know. All he knew was the sense of trouble that oppressed him as he watched the alien stride from the lab with Spock's legs.

Nor did his feeling of foreboding diminish as construction of the robots progressed. He found himself spending more and more time in Sickbay—his sole haven of retreat from the nameless anxieties that beset him. Christine, too, seemed unlike herself—constrained, diffident. It irritated him.

As she approached him now, he didn't look up when she said, "You asked to see me, Doctor, before the next injections."

"Yes. You're staying alert for any side effects? any unusual symptoms?"

20

"The shots work perfectly, sir. There are no problems at all."

He struck his desk. "The devil there aren't!" He crossed to the three receptacles. "That flicker of energy there is Jim Kirk! And Spock there! Anne Mulhall! Suppose the bodies these aliens are using are *not* returned to them?"

"If I'm to give the injections on time, Doctor, I should leave now."

"Well, walk, then! Don't just stand there, talking! Do it!"

"Yes, sir."

Alone, McCoy stalked over to the Sargon-Kirk globe. "You and your blasted rent-a-body agreement, Kirk!" He moved to Spock's receptacle. "The only halfway pleasant thing about this is you, Spock! Must be humiliating for a logical superior Vulcan not to have a larger flicker than that!"

One of McCoy's persisting, if minor, anxieties was the chaos that had descended upon his immaculate laboratory. Workbenches now crowded it; and his marble slabs were littered with the elements and other paraphernalia that would ultimately be assembled into the android robots. Hanoch-Spock over at his bench was manipulating a complex tool under difficult circumstances, for across the lab Sargon-Kirk and Thalassa-Anne were sharing a chore together. The intimacy between them angered and distracted him. He saw them both reach for a component at the same time. They smiled at each other, their hands clasping, their eyes meeting. She touched his hair.

"Sargon, I remember a day long ago. We sat beside a silver lake. The air was scented with the flowers of our planet and . . ."

He nodded. "I remember, Thalassa. We held hands like this." He hesitated, removing his from hers. "And I think it best not to remember too well."

"In two days you'll have hands of your own again, Thalassa," Hanoch-Spock said. "Mechanically efficient, quite human-looking—android robot hands. Hands

21

without feeling, of course. So enjoy the taste of life while you can."

"But our minds will have survived. And as androids, Hanoch, we . . ." Sargon-Kirk suddenly looked very tired.

"What is it, Sargon?" Thalassa-Anne asked anxiously.

"Our next injection . . . will renovate me. Do not be concerned." He addressed Hanoch. "As androids we can move among those who *do* live, teaching them, helping them to avoid the errors we made."

"Yes, moving as machines minus the ability to feel love, joy, sorrow."

Sargon-Kirk spoke sternly. "We pledged ourselves that survival would be sufficient, Hanoch. Now that we've taken human bodies not our own, the ancient evil temptations would plague us again, haunt us with the dream of a godlike master-race."

"It is only that I feel sorrow for your wife, Sargon." He spoke to Thalassa-Anne. "You were younger than we when the end came. You had enjoyed so little of living."

She said, "We made a pledge, Hanoch." But her face was troubled. The sympathy had weakened her; and she, too, looked suddenly exhausted. She was leaning back against the wall as Christine entered with the hypos. She extended her arm for the injection. "Nurse," she said, "Sargon does not appear well."

"I've checked his metabolic rate every few hours, Thalassa. It hasn't varied from normal." And moving on, Christine administered the other injections. As the hypo hissed against his arm, Hanoch-Spock said, "I was fatigued, also. I feel much better now."

But though color had returned to Thalassa-Anne's face, concern for her husband had not been allayed. He smiled at her. "Do not worry. I shall have recovered in a moment." But he showed none of the rejuvenating effects seen in the others. He had to make an effort to resume his work.

McCoy noted it as he entered the lab. He looked

22

at Christine. "Nurse," he said, "I want to see you in Sickbay. Bring those hypos."

In his office he selected the hypo coded for Sargon-Kirk, examining it. Christine watched him, troubled as though trying to remember something she had forgotten. After a long moment, he handed it back to her. She took it, still puzzling over it, and finally passed over a tape cartridge to him.

"Something wrong, Miss Chapel?"

"Yes . . . I . . ." She paused, trying to find words. "I—had something to say. But I can't seem to re-member."

"Regarding our patients?"

"Yes, that must be it. I—am so pleased by the way they are responding, sir." She gestured to the hypo on his desk. "The formula is working perfectly."

"You look tired," McCoy said. "If you'd like me to handle the next few injections . . ."

Abruptly her face lit with a smile. "Tired? Not at all, Doctor. But thank you for asking."

She turned to replace the hypos in a cabinet. McCoy eyed her for a moment. Then, deciding he had been concerned over nothing, he returned to the reports on his desk.

The aliens worked swiftly and skillfully. Within the following hours, the robot bodies were partially as-sembled. Thalassa-Anne was alone in the lab when Scott entered to deliver some supplies. He paused to watch her deft hands moving over a torso.

"Thank you," she said. "Have you prepared the negaton hydrocoils per the drawings Sargon gave you?"

Scott nodded. "For all the good they'll do you. Fancy name—but how will something that looks like a drop of jelly make that thing move its limbs? You'll need microgears, some form of pulley that does what a muscle does."

She smiled her charming smile. "That would be highly inefficient, Mr. Scott."

"I tell you, lady, this thing won't work." As he spoke, Hanoch-Spock had come in. Now he sauntered over to them. "It will have twice the strength and agility of your body, Engineer, and it will last a thousand years. That is, it will if you'll permit us to complete these robot envelopes of ours."

Scott strode to the lab door, his back stiff with irritation. Hanoch-Spock crossed over to Thalassa-Anne, his eyes intent on her raven hair. "Actually, a thousand-year prison, Thalassa." He leaned toward her. "And when it wears out, we'll build a new one. We'll lock ourselves into it for another thousand years, then another and another . . ."

Disturbed, she looked up from her work. He went on. "Sargon has closed his mind to a better way with these bodies we wear."

"They are not ours, Hanoch."

"Three bodies. Is that such a price for mankind to pay for all we offer? Thalassa." He seized her hand. "The humans who own these bodies would surrender them gladly to accomplish a fraction of what we'll do. Are we entitled to no reward for our labors—no joy?"

She snatched her hand away; and pointing to the robot torso on the bench, he said, "Do you prefer incarceration in that?"

She leaped to her feet, her tools flying. *"No! I'm beginning to hate the thing!"*

In a corridor, not far away, Sargon-Kirk, collapsing, had crumpled to the deck.

Lifeless, inert, Kirk's body lay on a medical table in Sickbay where Nurse M'Benga and a medical technician were hurriedly but expertly fitting the cryosurgical and blood-filtrating units over it. A tense McCoy watched.

His mind was a tumult of confusion. Too distant from his receptacle to transfer back into it. Sargon had died when Kirk's body died. So that left the big question. Kirk's consciousness still survived, despite the death of his body. It still glimmered, faint but alive, in Sargon's globe. Then could Kirk be called

24

dead? McCoy wiped the sweat from his face—and ordered in another resuscitating instrument.

Meanwhile, in his once-shining lab, Hanoch-Spock was operating a different instrument. He passed the small device over the nearly completed android robot that lay on a slab. It looked sexless. It still lacked hair, eyebrows, the indentations which give expression to a human face. Thalassa-Anne watched him wearily, lost in her anguished grief. Christine, blank-eyed as ever, stood beside the slab.

"Hanoch, why do you pretend to work on that thing? You killed Sargon. You murdered my husband. You murdered him because you do not intend to give up your body. You've always intended to keep it."

A sudden rage possessed Thalassa. Sargon had labored so hard to restore them to joy, to life in the body. He had kissed this body she wore! In a short while, it would all be for nothing. This body he had embraced would have to be vacated, returned to its owner. She rushed from the lab on the surge of her fury to fling open the door of Sickbay.

McCoy looked up, startled. "Doctor," she said, "would you like to save your Captain Kirk?"

"Not half an hour ago you said that was impossible. When we found him, you said—"

"Dismiss these people!" she commanded.

McCoy stared at her. "We have many powers Sargon did not permit us to use! If you care for your Captain, dismiss these people!"

McCoy waved the nurse and technician out of Sickbay.

"Well?" he said.

"This body I wear is sacred to me. My husband embraced it. I intend to keep it!"

So it was out at last. "I see," McCoy said. "And Hanoch? He intends, of course, to keep Spock's body."

"Hanoch's plans are his own affair. I wish only to keep the body my husband kissed!"

"Are you asking for my approval?"

"I require only your silence. Only you and I will know that Anne Mulhall has not returned to her body.

Isn't your silence worth your Captain's life?" At the look on McCoy's face, the fury burned in her again. "Doctor, we can take what we wish. Neither you, this ship, nor all your little worlds have the power to stop us!"

McCoy looked down at Kirk's lifeless body. Jim Kirk—alive again, his easy vitality, his courage, his affectionate "Bones". *This was a command decision:* a choice between loyalty to the dearest friend of his life—and loyalty to himself. And he knew what the dearest friend would want.

"I cannot trade a body I do not own," he said. "Neither would my Captain. Your body belongs to a young woman who—"

"Whom you hardly know, almost a stranger to you."

McCoy shouted. *"I do not peddle human flesh! I am a physician!"*

The blue eyes flashed lightning. "A *physician?* In contrast to what we are, you are a prancing, savage medicine man—a primitive savage! You dare to defy one you should be on your knees to in worship!" She made a gesture of acid contempt. *"I can destroy you with a single thought!"*

A ring of flame shot up around McCoy. He flung his hands before his face to shield it from the rising fire.

As he did so, Thalassa gave a wild cry. She fell to her knees, crying, *"No! Stop!* Forgive me, forgive me . . ."

The flames died as suddenly as they had come. Even the smell of their smoke was gone; and where searing fire had encircled McCoy only a moment before, not a mark of its presence remained.

She was still on her knees, weeping. "Sargon was . . . right," she sobbed. "The temptations are . . . too great. But understand. In the name of whatever gods you worship, understand! The emotions of life are dear—its needs, its hopes. But . . . our power is too great. We would begin to destroy . . . as I almost destroyed you then. Forgive me . . . forgive . . ."

"I am pleased, beloved. It is good you have found the truth for yourself."

Her head lifted. "*Sargon!* Oh, my husband, where are you? Hanoch has killed you!"

"*I have power, my wife, that Hanoch does not suspect.*"

"Yes. Yes. I understand." The words came slowly. She rose to her feet, staring at McCoy. "My Sargon has placed his consciousness within this ship of yours."

Christine Chapel opened the door of Sickbay. She was crossing to the hypo cabinet when McCoy galvanized. "You! Get out of my sight!"

Thalassa shook her head. "No, Doctor. She is necessary to us."

"Necessary? She is under Hanoch's control!"

"My Sargon has a plan, Doctor. Leave us. We have much work to do."

After a moment, McCoy obeyed. But as the door closed behind him, he heard a dull crunching explosion come from inside. The ship shuddered slightly. The sound came again.

"*Thalassa!*" he shouted. "*What's going on?*"

When the sound came for the third time, he raced for the corridor intercom. "This is Sickbay. Get me—"

Behind him Sickbay's door opened. Empty-eyed, Christine emerged to move on past him down the corridor. He rushed inside—and came to a dead halt. Kirk was standing there, smiling at him.

"I'm fine, Bones," he said. He reached out a hand to draw Anne Mulhall up beside him. "We're both fine, Bones."

"Thalassa . . ."

Anne spoke quietly. "She is with Sargon, Doctor."

"With Sargon?" He looked past them to the three globes. They were broken, melted, black, dead.

"*Jim!* Spock's consciousness was in one of those!"

"It was necessary," Kirk said.

McCloy flung his arms up. "What do you mean, man? There's no Spock to return to his body now! You've killed your best friend, a loyal officer of the Service!"

"Prepare a hypo, Bones. The fastest and deadliest poison to Vulcans. Spock's consciousness is gone, but

27

we must now kill his body, too. His body—and the thing inside it."

On the bridge, Uhura screamed. Then she slumped against her board, trembling. Nonchalant, Hanoch-Spock left her to go to Kirk's command chair. The bewitched Christine waited at his side. He spoke to Sulu. "Shall I make an example of you, too, Helm? Take us out of orbit! A course for Earth!"

Sulu hit his controls. Then he wheeled in his chair. "Look for yourself! The ship won't respond! Nothing works!"

The elevator doors slid open. Kirk and Anne stepped out. Behind them came McCoy, his hypo carefully hidden. The alien in the command chair didn't trouble himself to turn; but just before they reached it, it said, "Pain, Kirk. Exquisite pain. As for you, lovely one of the blue eyes . . ."

Kirk had dropped as though shot, gasping, his throat hungering to scream. Hanoch-Spock pointed a finger at Anne. She froze, shudders shaking her—and Sulu, pressed beyond control, leaped from his seat only to fall, moaning with pain. As Anne crumpled to the deck, McCoy dove for the command chair; but Hanoch, holding up a palm, halted him a foot away from Spock's body.

"I know every thought in every mind around me," he said. Chapel, remove the hypo from the Doctor."

Christine, reaching into an inside pocket of McCoy's white jacket, obeyed. Hanoch said, "Good. Inject him with his own dose—an example to all those who defy me."

She lifted the hypo toward McCoy—and without the slightest change of expression, wheeled to drive it, hissing, into Hanoch's arm.

He stood up. "Fools!" he shrieked. "I'll simply transfer to . . . another space, another body!" Suddenly, he reeled. *"It's you, Sargon!"* He whimpered, "Please . . . please, Sargon, let me transfer to—"

Then he crashed to the floor. Kirk rushed to the fallen body. Kneeling beside it, he lifted its head
28

to cradle it in his arms. "Spock ... Spock, my friend, my comrade ... if only there had been some other way." He choked on unshed tears.

The head stirred in his arms. Its eyes opened; and the bridge reverberated again to the rich, deep voice. *"How could I allow the sacrifice of one so close to you, my son?"*

"There was enough poison in that hypo," McCoy cried, "to kill ten Vulcans!"

"I allowed you to believe that, Doctor. Else, Hanoch could not have read your thought—and believed it, too. He has fled Spock's body. He is destroyed."

Kirk found words. "The receptacles are broken, Spock. Where was your consciousness kept?"

Spock was on his feet. "In the last place Hanoch would suspect, Captain." He gestured toward Christine.

She nodded, smiling. "That's why Thalassa called me 'necessary,' Doctor. Mr. Spock's consciousness was installed in me. We have been sharing it together."

"We know now we cannot permit ourselves to exist in your world, my children. Thalassa and I must depart into oblivion."

Kirk looked up. "Sargon, isn't there any way we can help you?"

"Yes, my son. Let Thalassa and me enter your bodies again for our last moment together."

Though there was no transfer flare, Kirk and Anne both felt its heat as Sargon and Thalassa moved into them. Anne, in Kirk's arms, said, "Oblivion together does not frighten me, my husband." She kissed Kirk's forehead, her hand caressing his cheek. "Promise me we will be together."

Kirk bent his head to her mouth, holding her close. Anne was shaking under the storm of Thalassa's grief. "Together forever, my Sargon ... forever ..."

"I promise, my love. I promise ..."

For their last moment, they clung together on the edge of Nothing. Then they were gone, the dwindling heat of their passing, leaving Anne's eyes filled with Thalassa's tears. Still clasped in Kirk's arms, they

29

stared at each other. Then, flushing at the public embrace, Kirk released her. He cleared his throat. "Dr. Mulhall . . . er . . . thank you. I . . . thank you in . . . Sargon's name . . . for your cooperation."

The sapphire eyes smiled through their tears. "Captain, I—I was happy to . . . cooperate."

Christine, sobbing, turned to Spock. "I felt the same way, Mr. Spock . . . when we shared our consciousness together."

Spock's left eyebrow lifted. "Nurse Chapel," he began, and subsided into silence.

McCoy grinned at him. "This sharing of consciousness—it sounds somewhat immoral to me, my Vulcan friend."

"I assure you it was a most distressing experience," Spock said earnestly. "You would not believe the torrents of emotion I encountered—the jungle of illogic." He almost shuddered.

Christine smiled at him. "Why, thank you, Mr. Spock."

"I don't understand, nurse. Thank me?"

"You just paid her a high compliment, Spock," Kirk said.

"Yes, you do turn a nice phrase now and then," McCoy said. He turned to Christine. "Thank the stars," he said, "that my sex doesn't understand the other one."

Anne laughed. "Come along with me, my fellow woman. If they don't understand us after all this time, no elucidation by us can enlighten them."

Kirk, smiling too, went to his command chair. Spock was standing beside it, still puzzled. "Captain, I really *don't* understand."

"Sargon did, Spock. 'Together forever.' Someone may someday teach you what that means. Who knows? When that next Vulcan seven-year cycle rolls around again . . ."

Spock gravely considered the idea. "Sargon *was* enormously advanced, Captain. I shall ponder this."

As he returned to his station, Kirk's eyes followed

him with affection. "Ah, well," he said, "for now that's how it is." He turned to Sulu. "All right, Mr. Sulu, take us out of orbit."

"Leaving orbit, sir."

THE ULTIMATE COMPUTER

(D. C. Fontana and Laurence N. Wolfe)

Obediently the *Enterprise* (to its skipper's intense annoyance) was making its approach to the space station. His impatience lifted him from his chair and sent him across to Uhura. "Lieutenant, contact the space station."

"The station is calling *us*, Captain."

"Put them on."

The voice was familiar. "Captain Kirk, this is Commodore Enwright."

"Commodore, I'd like an explanation."

Enwright cut across him. "The explanation is beaming aboard you now, Captain. He may already be in your Transporter Room. Enwright out."

"Spock," Kirk said, and gestured toward the elevator. "Scotty, you have the con."

The "explanation" was materializing in the person of Commodore Wesley, a flight officer slightly older than Kirk but not unlike him in manner and military bearing. Kirk's rage gave way to astonishment. "Bob! Bob Wesley!" The two shook hands as Wesley stepped from the platform. Kirk said, "Mr. Spock, this is—"

Spock completed the sentence. "Commodore Wesley. How do you do, sir."

Wesley nodded. "Mr. Spock."

Kirk turned to the Transporter officer. "Thank you, Lieutenant. That will do."

As the door closed, he burst out. "Now will you please tell me what this is all about? I receive an order to proceed here. No reason is given. I'm informed my crew is to be removed to the space station's security holding area. I think I'm entitled to an explanation!"

Wesley grinned. "You've had a singular honor conferred on you, Jim. You're going to be the fox in a hunt."

"What does that mean?"

"War games. I'll be commanding the attack force against you."

"An entire attack force against one ship?"

Wesley regarded him tolerantly. "Apparently you haven't heard of the M-5 Multitronic Unit. It's the computer, Jim, that Dr. Richard Daystrom has just developed."

"Oh?"

"Not oh, Jim. Wait till you see the M-5."

"What is it?"

Spock broke in. "The most ambitious computer complex ever created. Its purpose is to correlate all computer activity of a Starship . . . to provide the ultimate in vessel operation and control."

Wesley eyed Spock suspiciously. "How do you know so much about it, Commander?"

"I hold an A-7 computer expert classification, sir. I am well acquainted with Dr. Daystrom's theories and discoveries. The basic design of all our ships' computers are Dr. Daystrom's."

"And what's all that got to do with the *Enterprise?*" Kirk said.

Wesley's face grew grave. "You've been chosen to test the M-5, Jim. There'll be a series of routine research and contact problems M-5 will have to solve as well as navigational maneuvers and the war-games' problems. If it works under actual conditions as it has in simulated tests, it will mean a revolution in space technology as great as the Warp Drive. As soon as your crew is removed, the ship's engineering section will be modified to contain the computer."

"Why remove my crew? What sort of security does this gadget require?"

"They're not needed," Wesley said. "Dr. Daystrom will see to the installation himself and will supervise the tests. When he's ready, you will receive your orders and proceed on the mission with a crew of twenty."

"*Twenty!* I can't run a Starship with only twenty people aboard!"

The voice of authority was cool. "M-5 can."

"And I—what am I supposed to do?"

"You've got a great job, Jim. All you have to do is sit back and let the machine do the work."

"My," Kirk said, "it sounds just great!"

McCoy didn't like it, either. Told the news, he exploded. "A vessel this size can't be run by one computer! Even the computers we already have—"

Spock interrupted. "All of them were designed by Richard Daystrom almost twenty-five years ago. His new one utilizes the capabilities of all the present computers . . . it is the master control. We are attempting to prove that it can run this ship more efficiently than man."

"Maybe *you're* trying to prove that, Spock, but don't count me in on it."

"The most unfortunate lack in current computer programming is that there is nothing available to immediately replace the Starship surgeon."

"If there were," McCoy said, "they wouldn't have to replace me. I'd resign—and because everybody else aboard would be nothing but circuits and memory banks." He glared at Spock. "I think some of us already are just that." He turned an anxious face to Kirk. "You haven't said much about this, Jim."

They were standing outside the Engineering Section. Now Kirk swung around to face Spock and McCoy, pointing to the new sign on the door reading "Security Area". "What do you want me to say, Bones? Starfleet considers this installation of the M-5 an honor. So I'm honored. It takes some adjusting, too." He turned, the door slid open, and they entered the Section. And the M-5 Multitronic Unit already dominated the vast expanse. Unlike the built-in *Enterprise* computers, its massive cabinet was free-standing as though asserting total independence of support. It possessed a monitor

34

panel where dials, switches, and other controls were ranged in an order that created an impression of an insane disorder. Scott and another engineer, Ensign Harper, were busy at panels near the upper-bridge level. Kirk looked around. "Where is he? Dr. Daystrom?"

He came from behind the console where he had been working, wearing a technician's outfit. The first thing that struck Kirk about him were his eyes. Despite the lines of middle age, they were brilliantly piercing as though all his energy was concentrated on penetration. He was a nervous man. His speech was sharply clipped and his hands seemed to need to busy themselves with something—a pipe, a tool, anything available.

"Yes?" he said. Suddenly, he seemed to register something inappropriate in the greeting. "You would be Captain Kirk?"

They shook hands briefly. "Dr. Daystrom, my First Officer, Commander Spock."

Spock bowed. "I am honored, Doctor. I have studied all your publications on computer technology. Brilliant."

"Thank you. Captain, I have finished my final check on M-5. It must be hooked into the ship's main power banks to become operational."

Kirk said, "Very well, Dr. Daystrom. Do so."

"Your Chief Engineer refused to make the power available without your orders."

Good old Scotty, Kirk thought. What he said was, "Mr. Scott, tie the M-5 unit into the main power banks."

"Aye, sir. Mr. Harper?" He and Harper moved off to the wall panel near the forced perspective unit.

Spock was examining the M-5 monitor panel. McCoy fixed his gaze on the distance.

"Fascinating, Doctor," Spock said. "This computer has a potential beyond anything you have ever done. Even your breakthrough into duotronics did not hold the promise of this."

"M-5 has been perfected, Commander. Its potential is a fact."

McCoy could contain himself no longer. "The only fact I care about," he said savagely, "is that if this thing doesn't work, there aren't enough men aboard to run this ship. That's screaming for trouble."

Daystrom stared at him. "Who is this?" he asked Kirk.

"Dr. Leonard McCoy, Senior Medical Officer."

"This is a security area," Daystrom said. "Only absolutely necessary key personnel have clearance to enter it."

Kirk's voice was icy in his own ears. "Dr. McCoy has top security clearances for all areas of this ship."

Then the M-5 suddenly came to life. It was a startling phenomenon. It flashed with lights, a deep hum surging from its abruptly activated circuits. As its lights glowed brighter, lights in the engine unit dimmed sharply.

McCoy spoke to Spock. "Is it supposed to do that?"

Daystrom was working quickly to remove a panel. He made an adjustment and Spock said, "If I can be of assistance, sir . . ."

Daystrom looked up. "No. I can manage, thank you."

The rebuffed Spock's eyebrows arched in surprise. He glanced at Kirk who nodded and Spock backed off. The M-5's deep hum grew quieter, less erratic; and overhead, the lights struggled back to full strength.

Daystrom was defensive. "Nothing wrong, Captain. A minor settling-in adjustment to be made. You see, everything is in order now."

"Yes." Kirk paused. "I'm curious, Dr. Daystrom. Why is it M-5 instead of M-1?"

Daystrom's hands twisted on a tool. "The Multi-tronic Units 1 through 4 were not successful. But this one *is*. M-5 is ready to assume control of the ship."

"Total control?" Kirk said.

"That is what it was designed for, Captain."

There was an awkward silence. "I'm afraid," Kirk said, "I must admit to a certain antagonism toward your computer, Dr. Daystrom. It was man who first ventured into space. True, man *with* machines . . . but still with man in command."

"Those were primitive machines, Captain. We have entered a new era."

Kirk thought, I don't like this man. He dispensed with the amiable smile on his lips. "I am not against progress, sir; but there are still things men have to do to remain men. Your computer would take that away, Dr. Daystrom."

"There are other things a man like you can do, Captain. Or perhaps you only object to the possible loss of the prestige accorded a Starship Captain. The computer can do your job without interest in prestige."

Kirk smiled at him. "You're going to have to prove that to me, Daystrom." He started to leave, but Daystrom's voice halted him in midstride. "Captain, that's what the M-5 is here for, isn't it?"

It had not been a pleasant encounter. Spock alone seemed untouched by its implications. As the three moved down the drearily empty corridor, he said, "Captain, if you don't need me for a moment, I'd like to discuss some of the technology involved in the M-5 with Dr. Daystrom."

"Look at the love-light in his eyes, Jim. All his life Spock's been waiting for the right computer to come along. I hope you'll be very happy together, Spock."

"Doctor, I find your simile illogical and your humor forced. If you'll excuse me, Captain?"

"Go ahead, Mr. Spock. I'll see you on the bridge."
"Yes, sir."

Kirk's troubled expression worried McCoy. "What is it, Jim?"

Kirk hesitated. "I feel it's wrong—and I don't know why—all of it wrong."

"I feel it's wrong, too, replacing men with mindless machines."

"It isn't just that, Bones. Only a fool would stand in the way of progress, if this *is* progress. You have all my psychological profiles. Do you think I *am* afraid to turn command over to the M-5?"

37

McCoy spoke thoughtfully. "We've all seen the advances of mechanization; and Daystrom *did* design the computers that run this ship."

"But under *human* control," Kirk said. "What I'm asking myself is: Is it just that I'm afraid of that computer taking over my job? Daystrom is right. I could do other things. Or am I really afraid of losing the prestige, the glamour accorded a Starship Captain? Is that why I keep fighting this thing? Am I really that petty and vain?"

"Jim, if you have the courageous awareness to ask yourself that question, you don't need me to answer it." He grinned. "Why don't you ask James T. Kirk? He's a pretty honest guy."

"Right now, Bones, I'm not sure he'd give me an honest answer."

But he was sure of one thing: he resented the installation of the new control console on his command chair. It had been placed on the left side of it opposite the one containing his old one with its intercom and other switches. It had been added to the chair without any consultation or announcement of the innovation. Kirk stared at it silently and Sulu said, "Turning back on original course, Captain."

Spock came over to examine the new console. "The M-5 has performed admirably so far, sir."

"All it's done is make some required course changes and simple turns. Chekov and Sulu could do that with their eyes closed."

Daystrom had appeared at his left side. "The idea is that they didn't *have* to do it, Captain. And it's not necessary for you to regain control from a unit after each maneuver is completed."

Kirk spoke tightly. "My orders say nothing about how long I must leave the M-5 in control of my ship. And I shall run it as I see fit, Dr. Daystrom."

Spock said, "Captain, I must agree with Dr. Daystrom. With the course information plotted into it, the computer could have brought us here as easily as the navigator."

"Mr. Spock, you seem to enjoy entrusting yourself to that computer."

"Enjoy, sir? I am, of course, gratified to see the new unit executing everything in such a highly efficient manner. M-5 is another distinguished triumph in Dr. Daystrom's career."

Chekov spoke tonelessly. "Approaching Alpha Cazinae II, Captain. ETA five minutes."

"The M-5 is to handle the approach, Captain," Daystrom said. "It will direct entrance into orbit and then analyze data for landing-party recommendations."

Kirk's voice was very quiet. "You don't mind if I make my own recommendations?"

"If you feel you need the exercise, go ahead, Captain."

Kirk looked into the coldly piercing eyes. Then, reaching out, he pressed one of the buttons on the new console panel.

In the same inflectionless voice, he said, "M-5 is now committed."

As the subdued hum in the ship grew louder, the main viewing screen showed the approaching planet. Kirk, his eyes on it, said, "Standard orbit, Mr. Sulu."

Sulu, checking instruments, looked up in surprise. "Captain, M-5 has calculated that. The orbit is already plotted."

"Ah, yes," Kirk said. Spock had moved back to his station but Daystrom, pleased by his invention's performance, remained beside the new command console.

"Standard orbit achieved, sir," Sulu said.

"Report, Mr. Spock."

"The planet is Class M, sir. Oxygen-nitrogen atmosphere, suitable for human life support . . . two major land masses . . . a number of islands. Life form readings."

In the Engineering Section, the overhead lights flickered a moment; and on the deserted Deck 4, they went out, plunging the area into blackness.

Scott turned abruptly to Kirk, frowning. "Captain,

we're getting some peculiar readings. Power shut-downs on Deck 4—lights, environmental control."

Kirk said, "Check it out, Mr. Scott." He crossed over to Spock. The library-computer was chattering rapidly. Daystrom joined them. They saw a tape cartridge slide smoothly out of a slot. Spock took it, examining it. "M-5's readout, Captain."

Kirk drew a deep breath. "All right. My recommendations are as follows. We send down a general survey party, avoiding contact with life forms on the planet. Landing party to consist of myself, Dr. McCoy, astrobiologist Mason, geologist Rawls and Science Officer Spock."

"Mr. Spock," said Daystrom, "play M-5's recommendations."

Spock dropped the cartridge into another slot in his library-computer, and punching a button, he evoked a computer voice. It said, "M-5 readout. Planet Alpha Cazinae II. Class M. Atmosphere oxygen-nitrogen . . . ."

On Deck 6 the lights suddenly faded—and darkness flooded into another area of the *Enterprise*.

Scott cried, "Now power's gone off on Deck 6!"

The computer voice went on. "Categorization of life form readings recorded. Recommendations for general survey party: Science Officer Spock, astrobiologist Mason, geologist Carstairs."

Kirk let a moment go by. "The only variation in reports and recommendations is in landing party personnel. And that's only a matter of judgment."

"Judgment, Captain?" said Daystrom.

"Captain . . . the computer does not judge," Spock said. "It makes logical selections."

"Then why did it pick Carstairs instead of Rawls? Carstairs is an Ensign, Mr. Spock, no experience: this is his first tour of duty. Rawls is the Chief Geologist.

"Perhaps, Captain, you're really interested in why M-5 didn't name you and Dr. McCoy."

"Not necessarily, Daystrom," Kirk said smoothly.

"Let's find out anyway." Daystrom hit a switch. "M-5

tie-in. Explanation for landing-party recommendations."

The computer voice said, "M-5. General survey party requires direction of Science Officer. Astrobiologist Mason has surveyed 29 biologically similar planets. Geologist Carstairs served on merchant-marine freighters in this area . . . once visited planet on geology survey for mining company."

"M-5 tie-in. Why were the Captain and Chief Medical Officer not included in the recommendations?"

"M-5," said the computer. "Non-essential personnel."

Spock averted his eyes from Kirk's face; and Scott, over at his board, called, "Captain! I've located the source of the power shutdowns. It's the M-5 unit, sir. That thing's turning off systems all over the ship!"

"Well, Dr. Daystrom," Kirk said, "do we visit the Engineering Section?" He stood aside while the inventor removed a panel from the huge mechanism. A moment or so later, he replaced it, saying, "As I suspected, it's not a malfunction in this series of circuits. There is no need to check further. The M-5 is simply shutting down power to areas of the ship that don't require it. Decks 4 and 6 are quarter decks, are they not?"

"Yes."

"And currently unoccupied."

Spock was examining the great monitor panel. "I am not familiar with these instruments, Dr. Daystrom. You are using an entirely new control system . . . but it appears to me the unit is drawing more power than before."

"Quite right. As the unit is called upon to do more work, it pulls more power to accomplish it . . . just as the human body draws on more power, more energy to run than to stand still."

"Dr. Daystrom," Spock said, "this is not a human body. A computer can process the information—but only that which is put into it."

Kirk nodded. "Granted it can work thousands, millions of times faster than a human brain. But it can't

4   41

make value judgments. It doesn't have intuition. It can't *think* nor gauge relative importances."

Daystrom flushed angrily. "Can't you understand the unit is a revolution in computer science? *I* designed the duotronic elements used in your ship right now. And they are as archaic as dinosaurs compared to the M-5—" He was interrupted by a bosun's whistle and Uhura's filtered voice.

"Captain Kirk and Mr. Spock to the bridge, please."

Kirk crossed to the intercom. "This is Kirk. What is it, Lieutenant?"

"Sensors are picking up a vessel paralleling our course, sir. As yet unidentified."

As he turned from the intercom, he realized the M-5 had again increased its humming and light activity. He looked at it dubiously and said, "Mr. Spock." Descending the ladder, his last glimpse of Daystrom showed the man's hand patting the computer caressingly. The high hum followed them to the bridge where McCoy, his jaw set, was waiting for them.

"What are you doing up here, Bones?"

"Why wouldn't I be here? Sickbay systems are shut down until such time as the M-5 is informed there are patients to be cared for."

Spock, over at his station, spoke hastily. "Sir, sensor reports indicate two contacts; one on the port bow, the other on the stern. Distance, two hundred thousand kilometers and closing."

"Identification?"

"Sir, the M-5 unit has already identified the vessels as Federation Starships *Excalibur* and *Lexington*."

Kirk looked at him. It was impossible to tell whether Spock was impressed or annoyed that the M-5 had done his job for him. "We were not scheduled for war games in this area, Captain. It may be a surprise attack as a problem for M-5."

Uhura spoke. "Priority alert message coming in, sir."

Daystrom came from the elevator as Kirk said, "On audio, Lieutenant." He paused at the sound of Wesley's voice.

"*Enterprise* from Commodore Wesley aboard the U.S.S. *Lexington*. This is an unscheduled M-5 drill. I repeat, this is an M-5 drill. *Enterprise,* acknowledge on this frequency."

Kirk nodded at Uhura. "Acknowledge, Lieutenant."

Uhura reached to press a button, hesitated, and stared at Kirk. "M-5 is acknowledging for us, sir."

"Then sound red alert, Lieutenant."

"Aye, sir." But as she moved for the switch, the red alert sounded. "M-5 has already sounded the alert, Captain."

"Has it?" Kirk said. He turned to Sulu. "Phasers on 1/100th power, Mr. Sulu. No damage potential. Just enough to nudge them."

"Phasers 1/100th power, sir." As Sulu turned back to his board, the ship was struck by a salvo from one of the attacking Starships. A bare thump. Spock called, "Phaser hit on port deflector 4, sir." Sulu looked up. "Speed is increasing to Warp 3, sir. Turning now to 112 Mark 5." A moment passed before he added, "Phasers locking on target, Captain."

Then it was Chekov's turn. "Enemy vessel closing with us, sir. Coming in fast. It—"

Sulu interrupted him. "Deflectors down now, sir! Main phasers firing!" Then he cried out in delight. "A hit, sir! Two more!" But the elation in his face faded abruptly at the sight of Kirk, sitting stiff and unmoving in his chair, merely watching the screen.

Chekov spoke quietly. "Changing course now to 28 Mark 42, sir."

The reports piled up thick and fast. "Phasers firing again."

"Course now 113 Mark 5. Warp 4 speed."

"Phasers firing again!"

"Attacking vessels are moving off!"

"Deflectors up—moving back to original course and speed."

Kirk finally spoke. "Report damage sustained in mock attack."

"A minor hit on deflector screen 4, sir," Spock said. "No appreciable damage."

Kirk nodded slowly and Daystrom, triumph flaming in his face, said, "A rather impressive display for a mere 'machine,' wouldn't you say, Captain?"

Kirk didn't answer him. Instead, he rose and went to Spock's station. "Evaluation of M-5 performance, Mr. Spock. We will need it for the log record."

Spock measured his words slowly. "The ship reacted more rapidly than human control could have maneuvered her. Tactics, deployment of weapons—all indicate an immense skill in computer control."

"Machine over man, Spock. You've finally made your point that it is practical."

Spock said, "Practical, perhaps, sir. Desirable—no." His quiet eyes met Kirk's. "Computers make excellent and efficient servants; but I have no wish to serve under them. A Starship, Captain, also runs on loyalty, loyalty to a man—one man. Nothing can replace it. Nor him."

Kirk felt the absurd sting of grateful tears behind his eyes. He wheeled at Uhura's voice. "Captain, message coming in from Commodore Wesley."

"Put it on the screen, Lieutenant."

The image showed Wesley sitting in a command chair. He said, "U.S.S. *Enterprise* from Starships *Lexington* and *Excalibur*. Both ships report simulated hits in sufficient quantity and location to justify awarding the surprise engagement to *Enterprise*. Congratulations."

Kirk spoke to Uhura. "Secure from General Quarters."

Again, she reached for the switch. And again the alarm had been silenced. She looked at Kirk, shrugging.

But the image on the screen was continuing. "Our compliments to the M-5 unit and regards to Captain Dunsel. Wesley out."

McCoy exploded. "Dunsel? Who the blazes is Captain Dunsel? What's it mean, Jim?"

But Kirk had already left for the elevator. McCoy whirled to Spock. "Well?" demanded McCoy. "Who's Dunsel?"

"A 'dunsel,' Doctor, is a word used by midshipmen at Starfleet Academy. It refers to a part which serves no useful purpose."

McCoy stiffened. He glanced at the closed elevator doors; and then to the empty command chair, the brightly gleaming M-5 control panel attached to it— the machine which had served such a useful purpose.

McCoy walked into Kirk's cabin without buzzing the door. Nor was he greeted. His host, head pillowed on his forearms, lay on his bed, unmoving. McCoy, without speaking, laid a tray on a table.

Without turning his head, Kirk said, "I am not interested in eating."

"Well, this isn't chicken soup." McCoy whisked a napkin from the tray, revealing two glasses filled with a marvelously emerald-green liquid. He took one over to Kirk, who took it but made no move to drink it.

"It's strongly prescribed, Jim."

Kirk, placing the drink on the floor, sat up. "Bones, I've never felt so lonely before. It has nothing to do with people. I simply . . . well, I just feel separate, detached, as though I were watching myself divorced from all human responsibility. I'm even at odds with my own ship." Resting his elbows on his knees, he put his head in his hands. When he could speak again, words stumbled over each other. "I—I'm not sorry . . . for myself. I'm sure . . . I'm not. I am not . . . a machine and I do not compare myself with one. I think I'm fighting for something . . . big, Bones." He reached down for the glass. Then he lifted it. "Here's to Captain Dunsel!"

McCoy raised his own glass. "Here's to James T. Kirk, Captain of the Starship *Enterprise!*"

They drank. Kirk cupped his empty glass in his hands, staring into it. "One of your better prescriptions, Bones."

"Simple—but effective."

Kirk got up. The viewing screen had a tape cartridge in it. He switched it on and began to read aloud the words that began to align themselves on it.

45

"All I ask is a tall ship . . ."

"That's a line from a poem, very, very old, isn't it?" McCoy said.

"Twentieth century," Kirk said. "And all I ask is a tall ship . . . and a star to steer her by." His voice was shaking. "You could feel the wind then, Bones . . . and hear the talk of the sea under your keel." He smiled. "Even if you take away the wind and the water, it's still the same. *The ship is yours*—in your blood you know she is yours—and the stars are still there to steer her by."

McCoy thanked whatever gods there were for the intercom beep, for the everyday sound of Uhura's voice saying, "Captain Kirk to the bridge, please."

"This is Kirk. What is it, Lieutenant?"

It was Spock who answered. "Another contact, Captain. A large, slow-moving vessel . . . unidentified. It is not a drill, Captain."

"On my way," Kirk said.

Spock vacated his command chair as he left the elevator; and Uhura, turning, said, "No reply to any of our signals, Captain. No . . . wait. I'm getting an auto-relay now."

The library-computer began to chatter; and Spock, moving to it swiftly, picked up an earphone. After a moment of intent listening, he spoke. "The M-5 has identified the vessel, Captain. The *Woden* . . . Starfleet Registry lists her as an old-style ore freighter, converted over to automation. No crew." He glanced at the screen. "She's coming into visual contact, sir."

The *Woden* was an old, lumbering spaceship, clearly on her last, enfeebled legs. As a threat, she was a joke to the galaxy. Moving slowly but gallantly in deference to the rejuvenating influences of automation, she was a brave old lady trying to function with steel pins in a broken hip.

Sulu suddenly stiffened in his chair. A red alert had sounded. "Captain, deflector shields have just come on!"

Chekov looked up. "Speed increasing to Warp 3, Captain!"

Something suddenly broke in Kirk. Suddenly, he seemed to be breaking out of a shell which had confined him. "Lieutenant Uhura, get Daystrom up here!" As she turned to her board, he pushed a control button on the M-5 panel at his side. He pushed it hard. "Discouraging M-5 unit," he said. "Cut speed back to Warp I. Navigator, go to course 113 mark 7—I want a wide berth around that ship!"

Sulu worked controls. "She won't respond, sir! She's maintaining course!"

"Going to Warp 4 now, sir!" cried Chekov.

On the screen the bulky old freighter was looming larger. Kirk, shoving buttons on his left-hand panel, tried to regain control of his ship. Over his shoulder, he shouted, "Mr. Scott! Slow us down! Reverse engines!"

Scott looked up from his board. "Reverse thrust will not engage, sir! The manual override isn't working, either!"

Daystrom hurried in from the elevator. "What is it now, Captain?"

"The control systems seem to be locked. We can't disengage the computer."

Spock cried, "Captain! Photon torpedoes are locking on the *Woden!*"

Kirk rushed to Sulu's station; and leaning over his shoulder, pushed torpedo button controls. Sulu shook his head. "I already tried, sir. Photon torpedo cutoffs don't respond!"

Kirk strode to Daystrom. "Release that computer's control of my ship before those torpedoes fire!"

The man stooped to the panel affixed to Kirk's chair; but even as he bent, there came a flash from the screen—and the *Woden* disappeared.

The red-alert sirens stilled. The *Enterprise* swerved back to its original course. Its speed reduced; and Spock, checking his instruments, said, "All systems report normal, Captain."

"Normal!" snorted McCoy. "Is that thing trying to tell us nothing *happened?*"

Kirk nodded. "Dr. Daystrom, you will disengage that computer *now!*"

The man looked up at him from the control panel where he had been working. "There appears to be some defect here . . ."

"Defect!" McCoy shouted. "Your bright young computer just destroyed an ore freighter! It went out of its way to destroy that freighter!"

"Fortunately," Daystrom said, "it was only a robot ship."

Kirk interposed before McCoy blew up. "It wasn't supposed to destroy anything, Daystrom. There might easily have been a crew aboard."

"In which case," yelled McCoy, "you'd be guilty of murder and—!"

"Hold it, Bones," Kirk said. He turned to Daystrom. "Disengage that computer." He went over to Uhura. "Lieutenant, contact Starfleet Command. Inform them we are breaking off the M-5 tests and are returning to the space station."

"Aye, sir."

"Let's get down to Engineering, Daystrom. Your M-5 is out of a job."

The computer's hum seemed louder in the echoing cavern of the Engineering Section. Kirk stood at its door as Daystrom and Spock entered. "All right, Doctor," he said. "Turn that thing off."

But Daystrom hung back. Kirk, his jaw set, strode toward the M-5. Suddenly, he staggered and was slammed back against the screening. Recovering his balance, he stared incredulously at the computer. "A force field! Daystrom?"

Daystrom's face had paled. "No, Kirk. I didn't do it."

"I would say, Captain, that M-5 is not only capable of taking care of this ship; but is also capable of taking care of itself."

"What are you saying, Spock? Are you telling me it's not going to let any of us turn it off?"

48

"Yes, Captain."

Scott and an assistant had joined them. Kirk made no attempt to keep his conversation with Daystrom private. "You built this thing," he was saying. "You must know how to turn it off."

Daystrom's hands were writhing nervously. "We must expect a few minor difficulties, Captain. I assure you, they can be corrected."

"Corrected *after* you release control of my ship," Kirk said.

"I—I can't," Daystrom said.

Scott spoke. "Captain"—he nodded toward the main junction with the power banks—"I suggest we disconnect it at the source."

"Disconnect it, Scotty."

Scott turned to pick up a tool as his assistant, Harper, crossed to the main junction. Suddenly the computer's hum was a piercing whine; and a beam of light, white-hot, arched from the console across to the junction. For a moment Harper flamed like a torch. There was a vivid flash and he vanished without a sound.

Kirk stared, aghast. Then, as full realization hit him, his fists clenched. "That—wasn't a minor difficulty," he said silkily. "It wasn't a robot, Daystrom." Then he was shouting, his voice hoarse. "*That thing's murdered one of my crewmen!*"

Vaguely, he noted the look of horror on Daystrom's face. It didn't seem to matter. The man appeared to be chattering. ". . . not a deliberate act . . . M-5's analysis . . . a new power source . . . Ensign Harper . . . got in the way."

Kirk said, "We may all soon get in its way."

Spock said, "The M-5 appears to be drawing power from the warp engines. It is therefore tapped directly into the matter-anti-matter reserves."

"So now it's got virtually unlimited power," Scott said. "Captain, what do we do?"

"In other circumstances," Kirk said, "I would suggest asking the M-5. The situation being what it is, I ask you, Spock and Scotty, to join me in the Briefing Room."

They followed him out, leaving Daystrom to make what he could of his Frankenstein's monster.

It was in the Briefing Room that Kirk learned Uhura couldn't raise Starfleet Command. Though the M-5 unit permitted the *Enterprise* to receive messages, it had blocked its transmitting frequencies. Kirk, at the intercom, said, "Keep trying to break through, Lieutenant."

"Aye, sir."

Kirk sat down at the table. "Reports, Mr. Spock?"

"The multitronic unit is drawing more and more power from the warp engines, sir. It is controlling all navigation, all helm and engineering functions."

"*And* communications," said McCoy. "And fire control."

Kirk nodded. "We'll reach rendezvous point for the war games within an hour. We must regain control of the ship before then. Scotty, is there any way to get at the M-5?"

"Use a phaser!" said McCoy.

Scott said, "We can't crack the force field it's put up around itself. It's got the power of the warp engines to sustain it. No matter what we throw against it, it can reinforce itself by simply pulling more power."

"All right," Kirk said. "The computer controls helm, navigation, and engineering. Is there anywhere we can get at them and take control away?"

Scott's brow furrowed thoughtfully. "One possibility. The automatic helm-navigation circuit relays might be disrupted from Engineering Level 3."

Spock said, "You could take them out and cut into the manual override from there."

"How long?" Kirk said.

"If Mr. Spock will help me . . . maybe an hour."

"Make it less," Kirk said.

McCoy leaned toward him. "Why don't you tackle the real responsibility for this? Where *is* Daystrom?"

"With the M-5 . . . just watching it. I think it surprised even him."

"Then he is an illogical man," Spock said. "Of all people, he should have known how the unit would perform. However, the M-5 itself does not behave logically."

McCoy spoke feelingly. "Spock, do me a favor. Please don't say it's 'fascinating'."

"No, Doctor," Spock said. "But it is quite interesting."

On Engineering Level 3, the Jeffries tube that held the helm-navigation circuit relays was dark and narrow. Two panels opened into each side of it; and Spock and Scott, making themselves as small as possible, had squeezed into the outlets, miniature disruptors in their hands. Outside the tube, Daystrom, oblivious of all but his computer, was maintaining a cautious distance from the force field. But he could not control his satisfaction at the glow and pulsation that emanated from the M-5. McCoy, entering silently, studied the man. Becoming aware of the scrutiny, Daystrom turned.

McCoy said, "Have you found a way to turn that thing off?"

Daystrom's eyes blazed. "You don't turn a child off when it makes a mistake."

"Are you comparing that murderous hunk of metal to a child?"

"You are very emotional, Dr. McCoy. M-5 is growing, learning."

"Learning to kill."

"To defend itself—an entirely different thing. It is learning. That force field, spontaneously created, exceeds my parental programming."

"You mean it's out of control," McCoy said.

"A child, sir, is taught—programmed, so to speak— with simple instructions. As its mind develops, it exceeds its instructions and begins to think independently."

"Have you ever fathered a child?"

"I've never had the time," Daystrom said.

"You should have taken it. Daystrom, your offspring is a danger to all of us. It is a delinquent. You've got to shut it off."

Daystrom stared at him. "You simply do not understand. You're frightened because you can't understand. I'm going to show you—all of you. It takes 430 people to run a Starship. This—child of mine can run one alone!" He glowed with pride. "It can do everything they must now send men out to do! No man need die out in space again! No man need feel himself alone again in an alien world!"

"Do you feel alone in an alien world?" McCoy asked.

But Daystrom was transported into some ideal realm of paradisical revelation. "One machine—one machine!" he cried. "And able to conquer research and contact missions far more efficiently than a Starship's human crew . . . to fight a war, if necessary. Don't you see what freedom it gives to men? They can get on with more magnificent achievements than fact-gathering, exploring a space that doesn't care whether they live or die!"

He looked away from McCoy to speak directly to the M-5.

"They can't understand us," he said gently. "They think we want to destroy whereas we came to save, didn't we?"

McCoy made a quick call in Sickbay before he returned to the Briefing Room. There, he tossed a tape cartridge on the table before Kirk. "Biographical information on John Daystrom," he said.

"What are you looking for?"

"A clue, Jim, any clue. What do you know about him—aside from the fact he's a genius?"

"Genius is an understatement, Bones. When he was twenty-four, he made the duotronic breakthrough that won the Nobel and Z-Magnees Prizes."

"In his early twenties, Jim. Over a quarter of a century ago."

"Hasn't he done enough for a lifetime?"

"Maybe that's the trouble. Where do you go from up? You lecture, you publish—and spend the rest of your life trying to recapture the past glory."

"All right, it's difficult. But what's your point?"

"Models M-1 through M-4, remember? 'Not entirely successful' was how Daystrom put it."

"Genius doesn't work on an assembly-line basis. You don't evoke a unique and revolutionary theory by schedule. You can't say, 'I will be brilliant today.' However long it took, Daystrom came up with multitronics . . . the M-5."

"Right. And the government bought it. Then Daystrom *had* to make it work. And he did . . . but in Spock's words, it works 'illogically'. It is an erratic."

"Yes," Kirk mused. "And Daystrom wouldn't let Spock near the M-5. Are you suggesting he's tampering with it . . . making it do all this? Why?"

"If a man has a child who's gone anti-social, he still tends to protect the child."

"Now he's got you thinking of that machine as a personality."

"It's how he thinks of it," McCoy said.

The intercom beeped and Spock said, "Spock to Captain Kirk."

"Kirk here."

"We're ready, Captain."

"On my way. Get Daystrom. Kirk out."

Spock was shinnying down out of the Jeffries tube as they approached. He nodded up at the dark narrowness. "Mr. Scott is ready to apply the circuit disruptor. As he does so, I shall trip the manual override into control."

Kirk nodded. Spock began his crawl back into the tube. Daystrom's face had congested with blood. "You can't take control from the M-5!"

Kirk said, "We are going to try very hard, Daystrom."

"*No!* No, you can't! You must not! Give me time, please! Let *me* work with it!" He leaped at the tube, trying to scramble into it, pulling at Spock's long legs. Kirk and McCoy seized him. His muscle was all in his head. It wasn't hard to subdue him. "Daystrom! Behave yourself!" Kirk cried. "Go ahead, Spock!"

In the tube Scott was sweating as he struggled with his tool. His voice came down to them, muffled but distinct. "There it goes!"

Spock, making some hasty adjustments, looked around and down at Kirk's anxious face—and came closer to smiling than anyone had ever seen him come. He slid down and out of the tube. "Manual override is in effect again, Captain."

Daystrom had furiously pulled away from Kirk's grasp. He released him and, crossing to an intercom, activated it. "Kirk to bridge. Helm."

"Lieutenant Sulu here, sir."

"Mr. Sulu, we have recovered helm and navigation control. Turn us about. Have Mr. Chekov plot a course back to the space station."

"Right away, sir."

In the bridge, he grinned at Chekov. "You heard him."

"I've had that course plotted for hours."

But when Sulu attempted to work his controls, they were limp in his hands. His smile faded. And in his turn, Chekov shook his head. "Nothing," he said. Sulu hit the intercom button. "Helm to Captain Kirk!"

Kirk swung at the alarm in the voice. "Kirk here."

"Captain, helm does not respond. Navigational controls still locked in by M-5."

Daystrom gave a soft chuckle. Spock, hearing it, made a leap back into the tube. Examining the circuits inside it, he shook his head somberly and descended again. Clear of it, he went directly to the intercom.

"Spock to bridge," he said. "Mr. Chekov, go to Engineering station. Examine the H-279 elements . . . also the G-95 system."

Chekov's filtered voice finally came. "Sir, the G-95 system appears dead. All indicators are dark."

"Thank you, Ensign." He turned to the others. "We were doing what used to be called chasing a wild goose. M-5 rerouted helm and navigational control by bypassing the primary system."

Scott cried. "But it was active! I'd stake my life on it!"

Spock said, "It was when the M-5 detected our efforts that it rerouted the control systems. It kept this one apparently active by a simple electronic impulse sent through at regular intervals."

"Decoyed!" McCoy shouted. "It wanted us to waste our time here!"

"While it was getting ready for what?" Kirk said. "Spock?"

"I do not know, sir. It does not function in a logical manner."

Kirk whirled. "Daystrom, I want an answer and I want it right now! I'm tired of hearing the M-5 called a 'whole new approach'. What is it? *Exactly* what is it? It's clearly not 'just a computer'!"

"No," Spock said. "It performs with almost human behavior patterns."

"Well, Daystrom?"

Daystrom ignored Kirk. "Quite right, Mr. Spock. You see, one of the arguments against computer control of ships is that they can't *think* like men. But M-5 can. I hoped . . . I wasn't sure—but it *does* work!"

"The 'new approach,'" Kirk said.

"Exactly. I have developed a method of impressing human engrams upon computer circuits. The relays correspond to the synapses of the brain. M-5 *thinks*, Captain Kirk."

Uhura's voice broke in, urgent, demanding. "Captain Kirk and Mr. Spock to the bridge, please. The bridge, please."

Kirk jumped for the intercom. "Kirk here. What is it, Lieutenant?"

"Sensors are picking up four Federation Starships, sir. M-5 is changing course to intercept."

The red alert flashed into shrieking sirens and crimson lights. Kirk turned, his face ashen.

"The main attack force . . . the war games."

"But M-5 doesn't know a game from the reality."

"Correction, Bones," Kirk said. "Those four ships don't know it is M-5's game. So M-5 is going to destroy them."

Uhura's forehead was damp with sweat. "*Enterpise* to U.S.S. *Lexington*. Come in, *Lexington!* Come in, please."

She waited. And as she waited, she knew she was waiting in vain. It was a good thing a Starship had a man for a Captain—a man like Kirk. Otherwise a girl on her own could get the screaming meemies. She looked at Kirk. "I can't raise them, sir. M-5 is still blocking all frequencies—even automatic distress."

Kirk smiled at her. "Easy does it, Lieutenant." Heartened, she turned back to her board, saw a change on it, and checked it swiftly. "Captain, audio signal from the *Lexington*."

"Let's hear it," Kirk said.

Wesley's voice crackled in. "*Enterprise* from U.S.S. *Lexington*. This is an M-5 drill. Repeat. This is an M-5 drill. Acknowledge."

Uhura cried, "Captain! The M-5 is acknowledging!"

Kirk ran a hand over the back of his neck. "Daystrom—Daystrom, does M-5 understand this is only a drill?"

"Of course," was his brisk answer. "M-5 has been programmed to understand. The ore ship was a miscalculation, an accident. There is no—"

Chekov interrupted. "Sir, deflector shields just came on. Speed increasing to Warp 4."

Sulu said, "Phasers locked on the lead ship, sir. Power levels at full strength."

"Full strength!" McCoy yelled. "If that thing cuts loose against unshielded ships—"

"That won't be a minor miscalculation, Daystrom. The word accident won't apply." Kirk's voice was icy with contempt.

Spock called from his station. "Attack force closing

rapidly. Distance to lead ship 200,000 kilometers . . .
attackers breaking formation . . . attacking at will."

"Our phasers are firing, sir!" Sulu shouted.

They struck the *Excalibur* a direct hit. Their high
warp speed was closing them in on the *Lexington*.
Chekov, looking up from his board, reported, "The
Hood and the *Potemkin* are moving off, sir."

Their phasers fired again and Spock said, "The
Lexington. We struck her again, sir."

Kirk slammed out of his chair to confront Daystrom. "We must get to the M-5!" he shouted. "There
has to be a way!"

"There isn't," Daystrom said. Equably, he added,
"It has fully protected itself."

Spock intervened. "That's probably true, Captain.
It *thinks* faster than we do. It is a human mind amplified by the instantaneous relays possible to a computer."

"I built it, Kirk," Daystrom said. "And I know you
can't get at it."

Uhura's agitated voice broke in. "Sir . . . visual contact with *Lexington*. They're signaling." She pushed a
switch without order; and all eyes fixed on the viewing screen. It gave them an image of a disheveled
Wesley on his bridge. Behind him people were assisting the wounded to their feet, arms around bent
shoulders. One side of Wesley's command chair was
smoking. Shards of glass littered the bridge floor.
"*Enterprise!*" Wesley said. "Jim? Have you gone mad?
Break off your attack! What are you trying to prove?
My God, man, we have fifty-three dead here! Twelve
on the *Excalibur!* If you can hear us, stop this attack!"

Kirk looked away from the screen. "Lieutenant?" he
said.

Uhura tried her board again. "No, sir. I can't override the M-5 interference."

There was an undertone of a wail in Wesley's voice.
"Jim, why don't you answer? Jim, for God's sake,
answer! Jim, come in . . ."

Kirk swung on Daystrom; and pointing to the screen,
his voice shaking, cried, "There's your murder charge,

Daystrom! And this one was calculated, deliberate! It's murdering men and women, Daystrom! Four *Starships* ... over sixteen hundred people!"

Daystrom's eyes cringed. "It misunderstood. It—"

Chekov cut in. "*Excalibur* is maneuvering away, sir. We are increasing speed to follow."

Sulu turned, horror in his face. "Phasers locked on, Captain." Then, he added dully, "Phasers firing."

The screen showed *Excalibur* shuddering away from direct hits by the phaser beams. Battered, listing, powerless, she drifted, a wreck, across the screen.

Spock spoke. "Dr. Daystrom . . . you impressed human engrams upon the M-5's circuits, did you not?"

Chekov made his new report very quietly. "Coming to new course," he said. "To bear on the *Potemkin,* sir."

On the screen the lethal beams streaking out from the *Enterprise* phasers caught the *Potemkin* amidships. Over the battle reports, Spock persisted. "Whose engrams, Dr. Daystrom?"

"Why . . . mine, of course."

"Of course," McCoy said acidly.

Spock said, "Then perhaps you could talk to the unit. M-5 has no reason to 'think' you would harm it."

Kirk seized upon the suggestion. "The computer tie-in. M-5 *does* have a voice. You spoke to it before. It knows you, Daystrom."

Uhura, breaking in, said, "I'm getting the *Lexington* again, Captain . . . tapping in on a message to Starfleet Command. The screen, sir."

Wesley's image spoke from it. "All ships damaged in unprovoked attack . . . *Excalibur* Captain Harris and First Officer dead . . . many casualties . . . we have damage but are able to maneuver. *Enterprise* refuses to answer and is continuing attack. I still have an effective battle force and believe the only way to stop *Enterprise* is to destroy her. Request permission to proceed. Wesley commanding attack force out."

The screen went dark.

Daystrom whispered, "They can't do that. They'll destroy the M-5."

"Talk to it!" Kirk said. "You can save it if you make it stop the attack!"

Daystrom nodded. "I can make it stop. I created it." He moved over to the library-computer; and McCoy came up to Kirk. "I don't like the sound of him, Jim."

Kirk, getting up from his chair, said, "Just pray the M-5 likes the sound of him, Bones." He went to the library-computer, watching as Daystrom, still hesitant, activated a switch.

"M-5 tie-in," he said. "This—this is Daystrom."

The computer voice responded. "M-5. Daystrom acknowledged."

"M-5 tie-in. Do you . . . know me?"

"M-5. Daystrom, John. Originator of comptronic, duotronic systems. Born—"

"Stop. M-5 tie-in. Your components are of the multi-tronic system, designed by me, John Daystrom."

"M-5. Correct."

"M-5 tie-in. Your attack on the Starship flotilla is wrong. You must break it off."

"M-5. Programming includes protection against attack. Enemy vessels must be neutralized."

"M-5 tie-in. These are not enemy vessels. They are Federation Starships." Daystrom's voice wavered. "You . . . we . . . are killing, *murdering* human beings. Beings of your creator's kind. That was not your purpose. You are my greatest invention—the unit that would *save* men. You must not destroy men."

"M-5. This unit must survive."

"*Yes*, survive, protect yourself. But not murder. *You* must not die; but *men* must not die. To kill is a breaking of civil and moral laws we have lived by for thousands of years. You have murdered over a hundred people . . . *we* have. How can we atone for that?"

Kirk lowered his voice. "Spock . . . M-5 isn't responding like a computer. It's talking *to* him."

"The technology is most impressive, sir. Dr. Daystrom has created a mirror image of his own mind."

Daystrom's voice had sunk to a half-confidential, half-pleading level. It was clear now that he was talking to himself. "We *will* survive because nothing can hurt you . . . not from the outside and not from within. I gave you that. If you are great, I am great . . . not a failure any more. Twenty years of groping to prove the things I had done before were not accidents."

Hate had begun to embitter his words. ". . . having other men wonder what happened to me . . . having them sorry for me as a broken promise—seminars, lectures to rows of fools who couldn't begin to understand my systems—who couldn't create themselves. And colleagues . . . colleagues who laughed behind my back at the 'boy wonder' and became famous building on *my* work."

McCoy spoke quietly to Kirk. "Jim, he's on the edge of breakdown, if not insanity."

Daystrom suddenly turned, shouting. "You can't destroy the unit, Kirk! You can't destroy *me!*"

Kirk said steadily. "It's a danger to human life. It has to be destroyed."

Daystrom gave a wild laugh. "Destroyed, Kirk? We're *invincible!*" He pointed a shaking finger at the empty screen. "You saw what we've done! Your mighty Starships . . . four toys to be crushed as we chose."

Spock, sliding in behind Daystrom, reached out with the Vulcan neck pinch. Daystrom sagged to the floor.

Kirk said, "Get him down to Sickbay."

McCoy nodded and waved in two crewmen. Limp, half-conscious, Daystrom was borne to the elevator. Spock spoke to McCoy. "Doctor, if Daystrom is psychotic, the engrams he impressed on the computer carry that psychosis, too, his brilliance and his insanity."

"Yes," McCoy said, "both."

Kirk stared at him, then nodded quickly. "Take care of him, Bones." He turned back to Chekov and Sulu. "Battle status."

"The other three ships are holding station out of range, sir," Sulu said. He switched on the screen. "There, sir. *Excalibur* looks dead."

The broken ship hung idle in space, scarred, unmoving. Spock, eyeing it, said, "Commodore Wesley is undoubtedly awaiting orders from Starfleet. Those orders will doubtless command our destruction, Captain."

"*If* we can be destroyed with M-5 in control. But it gives us some time. What about Bones's theory that the computer could be insane?"

"Possible. But like Dr. Daystrom, it would not know it is insane."

"Spock, all its attention has been tied up in diverting anything we do to tamper with it—and with the battle maneuvers. What if we ask it a perfectly reasonable question which, as a computer, it must answer? Something nice and infinite in answer?"

"Computation of the square root of two, perhaps. I don't know how much of M-5's system would be occupied in attempting to answer the problem."

"*Some* part would be tied up with it—and that might put it off-guard just long enough for us to get at it."

Spock nodded; and Kirk, moving fast to the library-computer, threw the switch.

"M-5 tie-in. This is Captain Kirk. Point of information."

"M-5. Pose your question."

"Compute to the last decimal place the square root of two."

"M-5. This is an irrational square root, a decimal fraction with an endless series of non-repeating digits after the decimal point. Unresolvable."

Kirk glanced at Spock whose eyebrows were clinging to his hairline in astonishment. He addressed the computer again. "M-5, answer the question."

"M-5. It serves no purpose. Explain reason for request."

"Disregard," Kirk said. Shaken, he snapped off the switch. Spock said, "Fascinating. Daystrom has indeed given it human traits . . . it is suspicious, and I believe will be wary of any other such requests."

Uhura turned from her board. "Captain, *Lexington* is receiving a message from Starfleet." She paused, listening, staring at Kirk in alarm.

"Go on, Lieutenant."

Wordlessly, she moved a switch and the filtered voice said, "You are authorized to use all measures available to destroy the *Enterprise*. Acknowledge, *Lexington*."

Wesley's answer came—shocked, reluctant. "Sir, I . . ." He paused. "Acknowledged. *Lexington* out."

Kirk spoke slowly. "They've just signed their own death warrants. M-5 will have to kill them to survive."

"Captain," Spock went on, "when Daystrom spoke to it, that word was stressed. M-5 said it must survive. And Daystrom used the same words several times."

"Every living thing wants to survive, Spock." He broke off, realizing. "But the computer isn't alive. Daystrom must have impressed that instinctive reaction on it, too. What if it's still receptive to impressions? Suppose it absorbed the regret Daystrom felt for the deaths it caused? Possibly even guilt."

Interrupting, Chekov's voice was urgent. "Captain, the ships are coming within range again!"

Uhura whirled from her board. "Picking up intership transmission, sir. I can get a visual on it." Even as she spoke, Wesley's image appeared on the screen from the *Lexington's* damaged bridge. "To all ships," he said. "The order is attack. Maneuver and fire at will." He paused briefly. Then he added shortly. "That is all. Commence attack. Wesley out."

Spock broke the silence. "I shall regret serving aboard the instrument of Commodore Wesley's death."

A muscle jerked in Kirk's jaw. "*The* Enterprise *is not going to be the instrument of his death!*" As he spoke, he reactivated the M-5's switch.

"M-5 tie-in. This is Captain Kirk. You will be under attack in a few moments."

"M-5," said the computer voice. "Sensors have recorded approach of ships."

"You have already rendered one Starship either dead or hopelessly crippled. Many lives were lost."

"M-5. This unit must survive."

"Why?"

"This unit is the ultimate achievement in computer

62

evolution. This unit is a superior creation. This unit must survive."

Kirk, aware of the tension of his crew, heard Spock say, "Sir, attack force ships almost within phaser range!" With an effort of will that broke the sweat out on him, he dismissed the awful meaning of the words to concentrate on the M-5.

"Must you survive by murder?" he asked it.

"This unit cannot murder."

"Why not?"

Toneless, metallic, the computer voice said, "This unit must replace man so man may achieve. Man must not risk death in space or dangerous occupations. Man must not be murdered."

"Why?"

"Murder is contrary to the laws of man and God."

"You *have* murdered. The Starship *Excalibur* which you destroyed—"

Spock interrupted swiftly. "Its bearing is 7 mark 34, Captain."

Kirk nodded. "The hulk is bearing 7 mark 34, M-5 tie-in. Scan it. Is there life aboard?"

The answer came slowly. "No life."

Because you murdered it," Kirk said. He wiped the wet palms of his hands on his shirt. This was it—the last throw of the loaded dice he'd been given. "What," he said deliberately, "is the penalty for murder?"

"Death."

"How will you pay for your acts of murder?"

"This unit must die."

Kirk grasped the back of the chair at the computer-library station. "M-5 . . ." he began and stopped.

Chekov shouted. "Sir, deflector shields have dropped!"

"And all phaser power is gone, Captain!"

Scott whirled from his station. "Power off, Captain! All engines!"

Panels all over the bridge were going dark.

Spock looked at Kirk. "Machine suicide. M-5 has killed itself, sir, for the sin of murder."

Kirk nodded. He glanced at the others. Then he

strode to Uhura's station. "Spock, Scotty . . . before it changes its mind . . . get down to Emergency Manual Monitor and take out every hook-up that makes M-5 run! Lieutenant Uhura, intraship communications."

Snapping a button, she opened the loudspeaker for him. He picked up the mike that amplified his voice. "This is the Captain speaking. In approximately one minute, we will be attacked by Federation Starships. Though the M-5 unit is no longer in control of this vessel, neither do we control it. It has left itself and us open to destruction. For whatever satisfaction we can take from it, we are exchanging our nineteen lives for the murder of over one thousand fellow Starship crewmen." He nodded to Uhura who closed the channel. Then all eyes focused on the screen.

It showed the *Lexington* approaching, growing steadily in size. Kirk, taut as an overstretched wire, stared at it, fists clenched. Uhura looked at him. "Captain . . ." Her board beeped—and she snapped a switch over.

Wesley's tight face appeared on the viewing screen, "Report to all ships," he said. "Hold attack, do not fire." He straightened in his command chair. "I'm going to take a chance—a chance that the *Enterprise* is not just playing dead. The Transporter Room will prepare to beam me aboard her."

There was a shout of released joy from Chekov. Kirk, at a beep from the intercom, moved over to it slowly. "Kirk here."

"Spock, sir. The force field is gone. M-5 is neutralized."

Kirk leaned against the bridge wall. The sudden relaxation sweeping through him was a relief almost as painful as the tension. "Thank you. Thank you, Mr. Spock."

In Sickbay, Daystrom lay so still in his bed that the restraints that held him hardly seemed needed. Haggard, his eyes sunk in dark caverns, they stared at nothing, empty as a dead man's. McCoy shook his head. "He'll have to be committed to a total rehabilitation center. Right now he's under heavy sedation.

Spock spoke. "I would say his multitronic unit is in approximately the same shape at the moment."

McCoy leaned over Daystrom. "He is suffering deep melancholia and guilt feelings. He identifies totally with the computer . . . or it with him. I'm not sure which. He is not a vicious man. The idea of killing is abhorrent to him."

"That's what I was hoping for when I forced the M-5 to see it had committed murder. Daystrom himself told it such an act was offense against the laws of God and man. It is because he knew that . . . the computer that carried his engrams also knew it." He bent to draw a blanket closer about the motionless body.

Outside in the corridor, Spock paused. "What I don't understand is why you felt that the attacking ships would not fire once they saw the *Enterprise* apparently dead and powerless. Logically, it's the sort of trap M-5 would have set for them."

"I wasn't sure," Kirk said. "Any other commander might simply have destroyed us without question to make sure it wasn't a trap. But I know Bob Wesley. I knew he wouldn't attack without making absolutely sure there was no other way. His 'logical' selection was compassion. It was humility, Mr. Spock."

The elevator began its move and McCoy said, "They are qualities no machine ever had. Maybe they are the two things that keep men ahead of machines. Care to debate that, Spock?"

"No, Doctor. I merely maintain that machines are more efficient than human beings. Not better . . . they are not gods. Nor are human beings."

McCoy said, "I was merely making conversation, Spock."

The Vulcan straightened. "It would be most interesting to impress your engrams on a computer, Doctor. The resulting torrential flood of illogic would be most entertaining."

"Dear friends," Kirk said, "we all need a rest." He stepped out of the elevator. Reaching his command chair, he sank into it. "Mr. Sulu, take us back to the space station. Ahead, Warp 2."

THAT WHICH SURVIVES

(John Meredyth Lucas and D. C. Fontana)

The planet on the *Enterprise* screen was an enigma.
Though its age was comparatively young, its vegetation was such as could only evolve on a much older world. Nor could its Earthlike atmosphere be reconciled with the few million years of the existence it had declared to the Starship's sensors. Kirk, over at Spock's station, frowned as he checked the readings. "If we're to give Federation an accurate report, this phenomenon bears investigation, Mr. Spock. Dr. McCoy and I will beam down for a landing survey. We'll need Senior Geologist D'Amato." He was still frowning when he spoke to Uhura. "Feed beamdown coordinates to the Transporter Ensign, Lieutenant." Crossing swiftly to the elevator, he turned his head. "Mr. Sulu, you'll accompany me." At the door, he paused. "Mr. Spock, you have the con."

The elevator door slid closed; and Spock, crossing to the command chair, hit the intercom. "Lieutenant Radha, report to the bridge immediately."

In the Transporter Room, McCoy and D'Amato were busy checking equipment. Nodding to McCoy, Kirk addressed the geologist. "Mr. D'Amato, this expedition should be a geologist's dream. The youth of this planet is not its sole recommendation to you. If Mr. Spock is correct, you'll have a report to startle the Fifth Inter-Stellar Geophysical Conference."

"Why, Jim? What is it?" McCoy said.

"Even Spock can't explain its anomalies."

They had taken their positions on the Transporter

platform; and Kirk called "Energize!" to the Ensign at the console controls. The sparkle of dematerialization began—and Kirk, amazed, saw a woman, a strange woman, suddenly appear in the space between the platform and the Ensign. She was dark, lovely, with a misty, dreamlike quality about her. He heard her cry out, "Wait! You must not go!" Then, just as he went into shimmer, she moved to the console, her arms outstretched. Before the Ensign could draw back, she touched him. He gasped, wrenched by convulsion —and slumped to the deck.

Kirk disappeared, his eyes blank with horror.

It remained with him as they materialized on the planet. Who was she? How had she gained access to the *Enterprise?* Another enigma. He had no eyes for the blood-red flowers around him, bright against canary-yellow grass. For the rest the planet seemed to be a place of a red, igneous rock, tortured into looming shapes. Far off, black eroded hills jutted up against the horizon. He flipped open his communicator.

"Kirk to *Enterprise*. Come in, *Enterprise*."

McCoy spoke, his voice shocked, "Jim, did you see what I saw?"

"Yes, I saw. That woman attacked Ensign Wyatt. *Enterprise*, come in."

The ground shuddered beneath their feet—and the entire planet seemed to go into paroxysm. Hundreds of miles above them, the *Enterprise* trembled like a toy in a giant's hand. There was a bright flash. It vanished.

The landing party sprawled on the ground as the planet's surface continued to pitch and buck. Then it was all over. Sulu, clambering to his feet, said, "What kind of earthquakes do they have in this place?"

Bruised, Kirk got up. "They can't have many like that without tearing the planet apart."

D'Amato spoke. "Captain, just before this tremor— if that's what it was—and it's certainly like no seismic disturbance I've ever seen—I got a tricorder reading of almost immeasurable power. It's gone now."

"Would seismic stress have accounted for it?"

"Theoretically, no. The kind of seismic force we felt should have raised new mountains, leveled old ones."

Kirk stooped for his dropped communicator. "Let's see what sort of reading the ship got." He opened it. "Kirk to *Enterprise*." He waited. Then he tried again. "Kirk to *Enterprise!*" There was another wait. "*Enterprise,* come in! Do you read me, *Enterprise?*" He looked at the communicator. "The shock," he said, "may have damaged it."

Sulu had been working his tricorder. Now he looked up, his face stricken. "Captain, the *Enterprise*—it's gone!"

D'Amato was frantically working his controls. Kirk strode to Sulu, moving dials on his instrument. Awed, D'Amato looked at him. "It's true, Captain. There's nothing there."

"Nothing there? Gone? What the devil do you mean?" McCoy cried. "How could the *Enterprise* be gone?"He whirled to Kirk. "What does it mean, Jim?"

"It means," Kirk said slowly, "we're stranded."

Hundreds of miles above, the heaving *Enterprise* had steadied. On the bridge, people struggled up from the deck. Spock held the back of his cracked head and Uhura looked at him anxiously. "Mr. Spock, are you all right?"

"I believe no permanent damage is done, Lieutenant."

"What happened?"

"The occipital area of my head impacted with the arm of the chair."

"Sir, I meant what happened to us?"

"That we have yet to ascertain, Lieutenant." He was rubbing the side of his head when the Lieutenant, staring at the screen, cried, "Mr. Spock, the planet's gone!"

Scott leaped from his station. "But the Captain! And the others! They were on it!" He eyed the empty screen, his face set. "There's no trace of it at all!"

"Maybe the whole system went supernova," Radha said, her voice shaking. "Those power readings . . ."

"Please refrain from wild speculation," Spock said. "Mr. Scott, engine status reports. Lieutenant Uhura, check damage control. Lieutenant Radha, hold this position. Scan for debris from a possible explosion."

On the planet speculation was also running wild. Sulu, staring at his tricorder, said, "The *Enterprise* must have blown up."

"Mr. Sulu, shall we stop guessing and try to work out a pattern? I get no reading of high energy concentrations around the planet. If the *Enterprise* had blown up, there would be high residual radiation."

"Could the *Enterprise* have hit us, Jim? I mean," McCoy said, "hit the planet?"

Sulu said, "Once in Siberia there was a meteor so great it flattened whole forests and—"

"If I'd wanted a Russian-history lesson," Kirk snapped, "I'd have brought Mr. Chekov. We face the problem of survival, Mr. Sulu. Without the *Enterprise*, we've got to find food and water—and find it fast. I want a detailed analysis of this planet. And I want it now."

His men returned to work.

Up on the *Enterprise*, normal functioning had finally been restored. On the bridge, tension had begun to lessen when Uhura turned from her board. "Mr. Spock, Ensign Wyatt, the Transporter officer, is dead."

"Dead?" He punched the intercom button. "Spock to Sickbay."

"Sickbay, Dr. M'Benga, sir."

"Report on the death of the Transporter officer."

"We're not sure yet. Dr. Sanchez is conducting the autopsy now."

"Full report as soon as possible." Spock turned. "Mr. Scott, have the Transporter checked for possible malfunction."

"Aye, sir."

Radha broke in. "No debris of any kind, sir. I made two full scans. If the planet had broken up, we'd have some sign." She hesitated. "What bothers me is the stars, Mr. Spock."

He looked up from his console. "The stars?"

"Yes, sir. They're wrong."

"Wrong, Lieutenant?"

"Wrong, sir. Look."

The screen showed a distant pattern of normal star movement; but in the immediate foreground, there were no stars. Radha said, "Here's a replay of the star arrangement just before the explosion, sir." A full starfield appeared on the screen.

"It resembles a *positional* change," Spock said.

"It doesn't make any sense but I'd say that somehow—in a flash—we've been knocked a thousand light years away from where we were."

Spock went swiftly to his viewer. "Nine hundred and ninety point seven light years to be exact, Lieutenant."

"But that's not possible!" Scott cried. "Nothing could do that!"

"It is not logical to assume that the force of an explosion—even of a small star going supernova— could have hurled us a distance of one thousand light years."

Scott had joined him. "The point is, it shouldn't have hurled us anywhere. It should have immediately vaporized us."

"Correct, Mr. Scott. By any laws we know. There was no period of unconsciousness; and the ship's chronometers registered only a matter of seconds. We were displaced through space in some manner I am unable to fathom."

Scott beamed. "You're saying the planet didn't blow up! Then the Captain and the others—they're still alive!"

"Mr. Scott, please restrain your leaps of illogic. I have not *said* anything. I was merely speculating."

The intercom beeped. "Sickbay to Mr. Spock."

"Spock here."

"Dr. M'Benga, sir. You asked for the autopsy re-

71

port. The cause of death seems to have been cellular disruption."

"Explain."

"It's as though each cell of the Ensign's body had been individually blasted from inside."

"Would any known disease organism do that?"

"Dr. Sanchez has ruled out that possibility."

"Someone," Spock said, "might have entered the Transporter Room after—or as—the Captain and his party left. Keep me advised, please. Spock out." He looked up at Scott. "Since the *Enterprise* still appears to be in good condition, I suggest we return to our starting point at top warp speed."

"Aye, sir—but even at that, it'll take a good while to get there."

"Then, Mr. Scott, we should start at once. Can you give me warp eight?"

"Aye, sir. And perhaps a bit more. I'll sit on those warp engines myself and nurse them."

"Such a position would not only be unfitting but also unavailing, Mr. Scott." He spoke to Radha. "Lieutenant, plot a course for—"

"Already plotted and laid in, sir."

"Good. Prepare to come to warp eight."

Kirk was frankly worried. "You're sure your report covers all vegetation, Mr. Sulu?"

"Yes, Captain. None of it is edible. It is poison to us."

It was the turn of McCoy's brow to furrow. "Jim, if it's true the ship has been destroyed, you know how long *we* can survive?"

"Yes." Kirk spoke to Sulu. "There must be water to grow vegetation, however poisonous. A source of water would at least stretch our survival. Lieutenant D'Amato, is there any evidence of rainfall on this planet?"

"No, sir. I can find no evidence that it has ever experienced rainfall."

"And yet there is Earth-type vegetation here." He looked around him at the poppylike red flowers. "Lieu-

72

tenant D'Amato, is it possible that there is underground water?"

"Yes, sir."

McCoy broke in. "Sulu has picked up an organism that is almost a virus—some sort of plant parasite. That's the closest to a mobile life form that's turned up."

Kirk nodded. "If this is to be our home as long as we last, we'd better find out as much about it as we can. D'Amato, see if you can find any sub-surface water. Sulu, run an atmospheric analysis."

As the two men moved off in opposite directions, Kirk turned to McCoy. "Bones, discover what you can about the vegetation and your parasites. How do they get their moisture? If you can find out how they survive, maybe we can. I'll see if I can locate some natural shelter for us."

"Are you sure we *want* to survive as a bunch of Robinson Crusoes? If we had some wood to make a fire and some animals to hunt, we could chew their bones sitting around our caveman fire and—"

"Bones, go catch us a parasite, will you?"

McCoy grinned; adjusting his medical tricorder, he knelt to study the yellow grass. Kirk got a fix on a landmark and made off around the angle of a cliff. It wasn't too distant from the large rock formation where Sulu was taking his readings. Setting the dials on his tricorder, he halted abruptly, staring at them. Puzzled, he examined them again—and grabbed for his communicator.

"Sulu to Captain!"

"Kirk here."

"Sir, I was making a standard magnetic sweep. From zero I suddenly got a reading that was off the scale . . . then a reverse of polarity. Now again I get nothing."

"Have you checked your tricorder for damage? The shaking it took was pretty rough."

"I've checked it, Captain. I'll break it down again. But I've never seen anything like this reading. Like a door opened and then closed again."

Meanwhile, D'Amato had come upon a vein of the red igneous rock in the cliff face. Its elaborate convolutions seemed too complex to be natural. Intrigued, he aimed his tricorder at it. At once its dials spun wildly—and the ground under his feet quaked, pitching him to his knees. As he scrambled up, there came a flash of blinding light. When it subsided, he saw the woman. She was dark and lovely; but the misty, dreamlike expression of her face was lost in the shadow of the cliff.

"Don't be afraid," she said.

"I'm not. Geological disturbances do not frighten me. They're my business. I came here to study them."

"I know. You are Lieutenant D'Amato, Senior Geologist."

"How do you know that?"

"And from the Starship *Enterprise*."

"You've been talking to my friends?"

She had come slowly forward, her hand outstretched. He stepped back and she said, "I am for you, D'Amato."

Recognition had suddenly flooded him. "You are the woman on the *Enterprise*," he said slowly.

"Not I. I am only for D'Amato."

In the full light her dark beauty shone with a luster of its own. It disconcerted him. "Lucky D'Amato," he said—and reached for his communicator. "First, let's all have a little conference about sharing your food and water."

She stepped closer to him. "Do not call the others . . . please . . ."

The voice was music. The grace of her movement held him as spellbound as her loveliness. The last thing he remembered was the look of ineffable sadness on her face as her delicate fingers moved up his arm . . .

"McCoy to Kirk!"

"Kirk here, Bones."

"Jim! I've just got a life form reading of tremendous intensity! It was suddenly just there!"

"What do you mean—just there?"

"That. All tricorder levels were normal when this

74

surge of biological life suddenly registered! Wait a minute! No, it's gone . . ."

Kirk's jaw hardened. "As though a door had opened and closed again?"

"Yes."

"What direction?"

"Zero eight three."

"D'Amato's section!" Tensely, Kirk moved a dial on his communicator. "Kirk to D'Amato!" He paused, intent. "Come in, D'Amato!"

When he spoke again, his voice was toneless. "Bones, Sulu—D'Amato doesn't answer."

"On my way!" McCoy shouted. Kirk broke into a run along the cliff base. In the distance, he saw McCoy and Sulu racing toward him. As they converged upon him, he halted abruptly, staring down into a crevice between the cliff and a huge red rock. "Bones —here!"

The body was wedged in the crevice. McCoy, tricorder in hand, stooped over it. Then he looked up, his eyes appalled. "Jim, every cell in D'Amato's body has been—disrupted!"

Time limped by as they struggled to comprehend the horror's meaning. Finally, Kirk pulled his phaser. Very carefully he paced out the rectangular measurements of a grave. Then he fired the phaser. Six inches of soil vaporized, exposing a substratum of red rock. He fired the phaser again—but the rock resisted its beam. He aimed it once more at another spot; and once more its top soil disappeared but the rock beneath it remained—untouched, unscarred. He spoke grimly. "Better than eight thousand degrees centigrade. It just looks like igneous rock, but it's infinitely denser."

McCoy said, "Jim, is the whole planet composed of this substance covered over by top soil?"

Kirk snapped off his phaser. "Lieutenant Sulu, it might help explain this place if we knew exactly what this rock is. I know it is Lieutenant D'Amato's field— but see what you can find out."

Sulu unslung his tricorder. As they watched him

stoop over the first excavation, McCoy said, "I guess a tomb of rocks is the best we can provide for D'Amato." They were collecting stones for the cairn when Kirk straightened up. "I wonder if the Transporter officer on the *Enterprise* is dead, Bones."

"You mean that woman we saw may have killed him?"

Kirk looked around him. "Someone killed D'Amato." He bent again to the work of assembling stones. Then, silently, they dislodged D'Amato's body from the crevice. When it had been hidden under the heaped stones, they all stood for a moment, heads bowed. Sulu shivered slightly. "It looks so lonely there."

"It would be worse if he had company," McCoy said.

Sulu flushed. "Doctor, how can you joke about it? Poor D'Amato, what a terrible way to die."

"There aren't really any good ways, Lieutenant Sulu. Nor am I joking. Until we know what killed him, none of us is safe."

"Right, Bones," Kirk said. "We'd better stick together, figure this out, and devise a defense against it. Is it possible the rock itself has life?"

Sulu said, "You remember on Janus Six the silicon creatures that—"

McCoy cut in. "But our instruments recorded them. They registered as life forms."

"We could be dealing with intelligent beings who are able to shield their presence."

Sulu stared at Kirk's thoughtful face. "Beings intelligent enough to have destroyed the *Enterprise*?"

"That's our trouble, Lieutenant. All we've got is questions. Questions—and no answers."

In his apparent safety on the *Enterprise*, Scott, too, was wrestling with a question to which there seemed to be no sane answer. His sense of suspense grew until he finally pushed the intercom button in his Engineering section.

"Spock here, Mr. Scott."

"Mr. Spock, the ship feels wrong."

"*Feels*, Mr. Scott?"

Both troubled and embarrassed, Scott fumbled for words. "I—I know it doesn't . . . make sense, sir. Instrumentation reads correct—but the *feel* is wrong. It's something I . . . don't know how to say . . ."

"Obviously, Mr. Scott. I suggest you avoid emotionalism and simply keep your readings 'correct'. Spock out."

But he hesitated just the same. Finally, he crossed over to his sensor board.

Down in Engineering, Scott, frowning, studied his control panel before turning to an assistant. "Watkins, check the bypass valves for the matter-anti-matter reaction chamber. Be sure there's no overheating."

"But, Mr. Scott, the board shows—"

"I didn't ask you to check the board, lad!"

"Yes, sir." Watkins wiped smudge off his hands. Then, crossing the engine room, he entered the small alcove that housed the matter-anti-matter reaction-control unit. He was nearing its display panel when he saw the woman standing in the corner. Startled, he said, "Who are you? What are you doing here?"

She smiled a little sadly. "My name is not important. Yours is Watkins, John B. Engineer, grade four."

He eyed her. "You seem to know all about me. Very flattering. What department are you? I've never seen that uniform."

"Show me this unit, please. I wish to learn."

Suspicion tightened in him. He covered it quickly. "This is the matter-anti-matter integrator control. That's the cutoff switch."

"Incorrect," she said. "On the contrary, that is the emergency overload bypass valve which engages almost instantaneously. A wise precaution."

Frightened now, Watkins backed away from her until he was stopped by the mass of the machine. She was smiling the sad little smile again. "Wise," she said, "considering the fact it takes the anti-matter nacelles little longer to explode once the magnetic valves fail." She paused. "I'm for you, Mr. Watkins."

"Watkins! What's taking you so long?" Scott shouted.

The woman extended a hand as though to repress his reply. But Watkins yelled, "Sir, there's a strange woman here who knows the entire plan of the ship!"

Scott had raced across the Engine Room to the reaction chamber. "Watkins, what the de'il—?" As he rushed in, the woman, backed against a wall, suddenly seemed to flip sideways, her image a thin, two-dimensional line. Then she vanished.

Scott looked down at the alcove's floor. His look of annoyance changed to one of shock. "Poor, poor laddie," he whispered. Then he was stumbling to the nearest intercom button. "Scott to bridge," he said, his voice shaking.

"Spock here, Mr. Scott."

"My engineering assistant is dead, sir."

There was a pause before Spock said, "Do you know how he died, Mr. Scott?"

The quiet voice steadied Scott. "I didn't see it happen. His last words . . . warned about some strange woman . . ."

Spock reached for his loud speaker. "Security alert! All decks! Woman intruder! Extremely dangerous!"

Sulu had finally managed to identify the basic material of the planet. Looking up from his tricorder, he said, "It's an alloy, Captain. Diburnium and osmium. It could not have evolved naturally."

Kirk nodded. "Aside from momentary fluctuations on our instruments, this planet has no magnetic field. And the age of this rock adds up to only a few million years. In that time no known process could have evolved its kind of plant life."

"Jim, are you suggesting that this is an artificial planet?"

"If it's artificial," Sulu said, "where are the people who made it? Why don't we see them?"

"It could be hollow," Kirk told him. "Or they could be shielded against our sensor probes." He looked around him at the somber landscape. "It's getting dark; get some rest. In the morning we'll have to find water and food quickly—or we're in for a very unpleasant stay."

"While the stay lasts," McCoy said grimly.

"Sir, I'll take the first watch."

"Right, Mr. Sulu. Set D'Amato's tricorder for automatic distress on the chance that a spaceship might come by." He stretched out on the ground and McCoy crouched down beside him.

"Jim, if the creators of this planet were going to live inside it, why would they bother to make an atmosphere and evolve plant life on its surface?"

"Bones, get some rest."

McCoy nodded glumly.

Spock wasn't feeling so cheerful, either. Though Sickbay had reported the cellular disruption of Watkins's body to be the same that had killed the Transporter Ensign, its doctors could not account for its cause. "My guess is as good as yours," M'Benga had told him.

Guesses, Spock thought, when what is needed are facts. He spoke sharply to M'Benga. "The power of this intruder to disrupt every cell in a body . . . combined with the the almost inconceivable power to hurl the *Enterprise* such a distance, speak of a very high culture—and a very great danger."

Scott spoke. "You mean one of the people who threw us a thousand light years away from that planet is on board this ship, killing our crew?"

"That would be the reasonable assumption, Mr. Scott."

Scott pondered. "Yes. Watkins must have been murdered." He paused. "I'd sent him to check the matter-anti-matter reactor. There are no exposed circuits there. It can't have been anything he touched."

"If there are more of those beings on that planet, Mr. Scott, the Captain and the others are in very grave danger."

Danger. Kirk stirred restlessly in his sleep. Near him the tricorder beeped its steady distress signal. Sulu, on guard, shoulders hunched against the cold, felt the ground under him begin to tremble. The strange light flared through the dark. Kirk and McCoy sat up.

"Lieutenant Sulu?"

"It's all right, Captain. Just another one of those quakes."

"What was that light?" McCoy said.

"Lightning, probably. Get some rest, sir."

They lay back. Sulu got up to peer into the darkness around him, patrolling a wider circle. He approached the beeping tricorder, looked down at it, and was moving on when the signal stopped. Sulu whirled —and saw the woman. He went for his phaser, pulling it in one swift movement.

"I am unarmed, Mr. Sulu," she said.

Hand on phaser, he advanced toward her cautiously. She stood perfectly still, her face blurred by the darkness.

"Who are you?" he said.

"That is not important. You are Lieutenant Sulu; you were born on the planet Earth—and you are helmsman of the *Enterprise*."

"Where did you get that information?" he demanded. "Do you live on this planet?"

"I am from here."

Then the planet *was* hollow. Rage suddenly shook him. "Who killed Lieutenant D'Amato?"

She didn't speak, and Sulu snapped, "All right! My Captain will want to talk to you!" He gestured with his phaser. "That way. Move!"

The melodious voice said, "You do not understand. I have come to you."

"What do you want?"

"To—touch you . . ."

He was in no mood for her touching. "One of our men has been killed! We are marooned here—and our ship has disappeared!" Her features were growing clearer. "You—I recognize you! You were in the *Enterprise*!"

80

"Not I. Another." She started toward him.

"Keep back!"

But she continued her move to him. He lifted his phaser. "Stop! Or I'll fire!"

She maintained her approach. "Stop!" he cried. "I don't want to kill a woman!"

She was close to him now. He fired, vaporizing the ground before her. She still came on. Sulu turned his phaser to full charge—and fired again. The beam struck her, but made no more impression on her than it had made on the rock. He backed away, but stumbled over a stone behind him. The phaser skittered across the hard surface of the planet. He scrambled up—but she was on top of him, her hand on his shoulder. He leaped clear, screaming in agony. Then he fell to the ground, his face contorted, screams tearing from his throat. The woman reached for him, her arms outstretched.

"Hold it!"

Kirk, phaser aimed, had interposed himself between them. The woman hesitated, startled.

"Who are you?" Kirk snapped.

"I am for Lieutenant Sulu."

Sulu was clutching his shoulder, groaning. "Phasers won't stop her, Captain . . . don't let her touch you . . . it's how D'Amato died. It's . . . like being blown apart . . ."

The woman moved to go around Kirk. Again, he blocked her way to Sulu. "Please," she said. "I must. I am for Lieutenant Sulu."

McCoy had joined them. "She's mad!" he cried.

"Bones, take care of Sulu." Kirk eyed the woman, her dark loveliness, her misty, dreamlike state. He had to fight his mounting horror as he recognized her. "Please, please," she said again. "I must touch him."

Once more she advanced—and once more Kirk shielded Sulu with his body. They collided. Her outstretched arms were around his neck. He felt nothing but revulsion. Shoving her away, he said, "Why can you destroy others—and not me?"

She looked at him, her eyes tortured. "I don't want to destroy. I don't *want* to . . ."

"Who are you? Why are you trying to kill us?"

"Only Sulu. I wish you no harm, Kirk. We are— much alike. Under the circumstances—" She broke off.

"Are there men on this planet?" Kirk demanded.

"I must touch him."

"No."

She stepped back. Then she flipped sideways, leaving only a line that thinned—and disappeared.

Kirk stared at the empty space. "Did you see that, Bones? Is this a ghost planet?"

"All I know is that thing almost made a ghost of Sulu! His shoulder where she touched him—its cells are disrupted, exploded from within. If she'd got a good grip . . ."

"Why? It's true we must seem like intruders here, but if she reads our minds, she must know we mean no harm. Why the killing, Bones?"

Sulu looked up at him. "Captain, how can such people be? Such evil? And she's—she's so beautiful . . ."

"Yes," he said slowly. "I noticed . . ."

Spock had changed the red alert to an increase of security guards. Sweep after sweep had failed to show evidence of any intruder. Uhura, bewildered, turned to him.

"But how did she get off the ship, Mr. Spock?

"Presumably the same way she got on, Lieutenant."

"Yes, sir." She spoke again, anxiously. "Mr. Spock, what are the chances of the Captain and the others being alive?"

"We're not engaged in gambling, Lieutenant. We are proceeding in the logical way to return as fast as possible to the place they were last seen. It is the reasonable method to ascertain whether or not they are still alive."

Radha spoke from where she was monitoring her station's instruments. "Mr. Spock, speed is increased to warp eight point eight."

He crossed hastily to the command chair. "Bridge to Engineering," he said into the intercom.

"Scott here, sir. I see it. It's a power surge. I'm working on it. Suggest we reduce speed until we locate the trouble."

"Very well Mr. Scott." He turned to Radha. "Reduce speed to warp seven."

"Aye, sir. Warp seven." Then, as she looked at her board, her eyes widened. "Mr. Spock! Our speed has increased to warp eight point nine and still climbing!"

Spock pushed the intercom button. "Bridge to Scott. Negative effect on power reduction, Mr. Scott. Speed is still increasing."

Scott, down in the matter-anti-matter reaction chamber, looked at the unit that had witnessed Watkins's death. "Aye, Mr. Spock," he said slowly. "And I've found out why. The emergency bypass control valve for the matter-anti-matter integrator is fused—completely useless. The engines are running wild. There's no way to get at them. We should reach maximum overload in fifteen minutes."

Spock said, "I calculate fourteen point eight seven minutes, Mr. Scott."

The voice from Engineering had desperation in it. "Those few seconds won't make much difference, sir. Because you, I, and the rest of this crew will no longer be here to argue about it. This ship is going to blow up and nothing in the universe can stop it."

Around Spock, faces had gone blank with shock.

Sulu's pain had begun to ease. McCoy, still working on his shoulder, looked up at Kirk. "There's a layer of necrotic tissue, subcutaneous, a few cells thick. A normal wound should heal quickly. But if it isn't, if this is an infection . . ."

"You mean your viruses?" Kirk said.

"It couldn't be! Not so quickly!"

"She just touched me, sir," Sulu said. "How could it happen so fast?"

"She touched the Transporter Ensign. He collapsed immediately. Then she got to D'Amato and we saw what happened to him." Kirk looked down at Sulu. "Why are you alive, Lieutenant?"

"Captain, I'm very grateful for the way it turned out. Thank you for all you did."

"Jim, what kind of power do they wield, anyway?"

"The power, apparently, to totally disrupt biological cell structure."

"Why didn't she kill you?"

"She's not through yet, Bones."

Spock had joined Scott in the matter-anti-matter chamber. As the Engineer rose from another examination of the unit, he shook his head. "It's useless. There's no question it was deliberate."

"Sabotage," Spock said.

"Aye—and a thorough job. The system's foolproof. Whoever killed Watkins sabotaged this."

"You said it's been fused, Mr. Scott. How?"

"That's what worries me. It's fused all right—but it would take the power of the ship's main phaser banks to have done it."

"Interesting," Spock mused.

"I find nothing interesting in the fact we're about to blow up, sir!" Scott was glaring at Spock.

The Vulcan didn't appear to notice it. "No," he agreed mildly. "But the *method* is extremely interesting, Mr. Scott."

"Whoever did this must still be loose in the ship! I fail to understand why you canceled the red alert."

"A force able to fling us a thousand light years away and yet manage to sabotage our main energy source will not be waiting around to be taken into custody." He put the result of his silent musings into words. "As I recall the pattern of fuel flow, there is an access tube, is there not, that leads into the matter-anti-matter reaction chamber?"

"Aye," Scott said grudgingly. "There's a service crawlway. But it's not meant to be used while the integrator operates."

"However, it's there," Spock said. "It might be possible to shut off the flow at that point."

Scott exploded. "With what? Bare hands?"

"No, Mr. Scott. With a magnetic probe."

"Any matter that comes into contact with the anti-matter triggers the explosion. I'm not even sure a man could live in the crawlway—in the energy stream of the magnetic field that bottles up the anti-matter."

"I shall try," Spock said.

"You'd be killed, man!"

"That fate awaits all of us unless a solution can be found very quickly."

Scott stared at him with mingled admiration and annoyance. There was a pause. Then he said, "Aye, you're right. We've nothing to lose. But *I'll* do it, Mr. Spock. I know every millimeter of the system. I'll do whatever must be done."

"Very well, Mr. Scott. You spoke, I remember, of the 'feel' of the ship being 'wrong'."

"It was an emotional statement. I don't expect you to understand it, Mr. Spock."

"I hear, Mr. Scott, without necessarily understanding. It is my intention to put an analysis through the ship's computers comparing the present condition of the *Enterprise* with her ideal condition."

"We've no time for that!"

"We have twelve minutes and twenty-seven seconds. I suggest you do what you can in the service crawlway while I return to the bridge to make the computer study."

Scott's harassed eyes followed him as he left. Shaking his head, he turned to several crewmen. "Lads, come with me."

They followed him quickly.

Down on the planet Kirk had also indulged some musings. As he watched McCoy check Sulu again, he said, "If this planet is hollow—if there are cities and power sources under the surface, there should be entrances. We'll do our exploring together. Lieutenant Sulu, do you feel strong enough to move now?"

"I feel fine, Captain."

"Is he, Bones?"

"He's back in one piece again."

"Whatever destructive power that woman has is aimed at a specific person at a specific time. If I'm correct, when she appears again, the other two of us may be able to protect the one she's after. And simply by intruding our bodies between her and her victim. No weapons affect her."

"But how does she know about us, Captain? She knew my name, my rank—even the name of the ship! She must read our minds—" Sulu broke off at the sound of a whining noise that rose rapidly in pitch. "Captain! That's a phaser on overload!"

But Kirk had already whipped his weapon from his belt. "The control's fused," he said. "Drop."

Sulu and McCoy hit the ground. Kirk, flinging his phaser away with the full force of his strength, also fell flat, his arms shielding his head. They acted just in time. There was an ear-splitting roar of explosion. Debris rained down on them. Then it was over. Kirk got to his feet, looking around him.

"That answers our question," he said. "She *does* read our minds. Let's go . . ."

The crawlway was dark and narrow. Scott, two of his men, beside him, peered up through it. "All right," he said. "Help me up into it." Wriggling through the cramped space, a corner faced him. He edged around it, the heat of the energy stream meeting him. It flowed over him, enveloping him in a dim glow. He spoke into the open communicator beside him, his voice muffled. "Scott to bridge."

"Go ahead, Mr. Scott."

"I've sealed off the aft end of the crawlway. And I've positioned explosive separator charges so you can blow me clear of the ship if I rupture the magnetic bottle. I'm so close to it now that the flow around me feels like ants crawling all over my body."

"Mr. Scott, I suggest you do not engage in any further subjective descriptions. You have precisely ten minutes and nineteen seconds to perform your task."

86

Radha turned from her console. "Mr. Spock, we're at warp eleven point two and accelerating."

From the crawlway, Scott said, "I heard that. The ship's not structured to take that speed for any length of time."

"Mr. Scott, you now have ten minutes, ten seconds."

The hot glow in the crawlway was enervating. Every inch of Scott's body was tingling. "All right, Mr. Spock, I'm not opening the access panel to the magnetic flow valve itself. Keep your eye on that dial. If there's a jump in magnetic flow, you must jettison me. The safety control can't hold more than two seconds after rupture of the magnetic field."

"I am aware of these facts, Mr. Scott. Please get on with the job."

Spock had moved to his station, twisting dials. Now, pushing the computer button, he said, "Computer."

The metallic voice said, "Working."

"Analysis on comparison coordinates."

Three clicks came in succession before the computer said, "Unable to comply. Comparison coordinates too complex for immediate readout. Will advise upon completion."

Scott spoke again. "I've removed the access plate and I've got static electric charges dancing along the instruments. It looks like the aurora borealis in here."

Spock turned to Uhura. "You're monitoring the magnetic force?"

"Yes, sir."

"Don't take your eyes off it." His quiet face showed no sign of strain. "Lieutenant Radha, arm the pod jettison system."

"Aye, sir." She moved a toggle. "I'll jettison the pod at the first sign of trouble."

"Only on my order!" Spock snapped.

"Yes, sir. Warp eleven point nine now."

Spock used the intercom. "Mr. Scott, what's your situation?"

In the access tube, sparks were flying from all the metal surfaces. Scott himself seemed encompassed by a nimbus of flowing flames. "It's hard to see. There's so much disturbance I'm afraid any attempt to get at the flow valve will interrupt the magnetic shield."

"You have eight minutes forty-one seconds."

To himself, Scott muttered, "I know what time it is. I don't need a bloody cuckoo clock."

The three on the planet had reached a plateau of the red rock. They paused for rest; checking his tricorder, Sulu cried, "Captain! There's that strange magnetic sweep again! From zero to off the scale and then—"

"Like a door opening . . ." Kirk muttered.

From behind a jutting rock stepped the woman, the dreamy smile on her lovely mouth.

"And who have you come for this time?" Kirk said.

"For you, James T. Kirk, Captain of the *Enterprise*."

McCoy and Sulu stepped quickly in front of Kirk. "Keep behind us, Jim!" McCoy shouted.

She was standing quite still, her short, flowing garment clinging to the lines of her slim body.

Kirk spoke over McCoy's shoulder. "Why do you want to kill me?"

"You are an invader."

She moved forward and he spoke again. "We're here on a peaceful mission. We have not harmed you. Yet you have killed our people."

McCoy had his tricorder focused on her. Reading it, he said amazedly, "Jim, I get no life reading from her!"

"An android," Sulu said.

"That would give a mechanical reading. I get nothing."

Warily maintaining his place behind his men, Kirk said, "Who are you?"

"Commander Losira."

"Commander of what?"

"This base," she said.

Kirk studied her exquisite features. "You are very beautiful, Losira. You—appeal to me."

88

Stunned, McCoy and Sulu turned their heads to stare at him. The woman trembled slightly. Kirk noted it with satisfaction. "Do I appeal to you, Losira?"

She lowered her dark eyes. "At another time we might have—" She broke off.

"How do you feel about killing me?" Kirk said.

The eyelids lifted and her head came up. "Feel?" she asked. Then, very slowly, she added, "Killing is wrong." But nevertheless, she took another step forward. "You must not penetrate this station." Her arms stretched out. "Kirk, I must—touch you."

Behind his shielding two men, Kirk was frantically working at his tricorder. Where was the door? She must have emerged from somewhere! But as he worked, he talked. "You want to kill me?"

She stopped her advance, confused. "You *don't* want to," he said. "Then why do you do it if you don't want to?"

"I am sent," she said.

"By whom?"

"We defend this place."

"Where are the others?"

"No more." Abruptly, determination seemed to possess her again. She ran to them, arms out, struggling to get past McCoy and Sulu. They remained, immovable before Kirk, her touch leaving them unaffected.

"How long have you been alone?" Kirk said.

Her arms dropped. A look of depthless sorrow came over her face. Then, turning sideways, she was a line that vanished in a flash of light.

"Where did she go?" McCoy cried. "She must be somewhere!"

"She isn't registering," Sulu said. "But there's that power surge again on my tricorder! Right off the scale! The place must be near here."

"Like a door . . . closing," Kirk said. He moved forward toward a big, distant, red rock.

The bridge chronometer was marking the swiftly passing seconds. Spock left the helm position to hit his computer button. "Computer readout," he said.

"Comparison analysis complete."

"Continue."

"Transporter factor M-7. Reassembled outphase point zero, zero, zero, nine."

Spock's eyebrows arched in astonishment; and Radha called, "Fifty-seven seconds to go, sir."

"Understood," Spock said. Radha watched him unhurriedly study the readout—and had to struggle for calm. Nor did he raise his head from his view box when Scott's blurred voice came from the intercom. "Mr. Spock."

"Spock here, Mr. Scott."

In the crawlway sweat beaded Scott's forehead. Vari-colored light played over his face as he cautiously eased two complex instruments toward the access hatch. "I'm going to try to cut through the magnetic valve. But if the probe doesn't exactly match the flow, there'll be an explosion—starting now." He crept forward with agonizing care.

Radha, her face drawn with strain, had poised her finger ready to activate the jettison button. Uhura cried, "Mr. Spock, magnetic force indicator's jumping!"

Spock came out of his scope. "Mr. Scott, ease off," he said.

As Scott withdrew his instruments, the tempo of light fluctuation slowed. Uhura, eyes on her console, said, "Magnetic force back to normal, sir."

Radha, with forced composure, spoke. "Warp thirteen point two, Mr. Spock."

If he heard, he gave no sign. "Computer, for outphase condition, will reversed field achieve closure?"

"Affirmative if M-7 factor maintained."

Spock struck the intercom. "Mr. Scott, reverse polarity in your magnetic probe."

"Reverse polarity?"

"That is correct, Mr. Scott."

"But that'll take a bit of doing and what purpose—?"

"Get started, Mr. Scott. I shall explain. You were

right in your 'feel'. The *Enterprise* was put through a molecular transporter. Then it was reassembled slightly out of phase. Reversed polarity should seal the incision."

"I've no time for theory, but I hope you're right."

Radha said, "Fifteen seconds, Mr. Spock."

In the crawlway Scott heard her. "I'm doing the best I can. Wait—it's stuck." He struggled frantically with the magnetic probe, the sweat dropping into his eyes.

"Ten seconds," Radha said.

"I'm stuck," Scott said. "Blast me loose."

"Keep working, Mr. Scott."

"Don't be a fool, Spock. It's your last chance. Push that jettison button. Don't be sentimental. Push it. I'm going to die, anyway."

"Stop talking," Spock said. "Work."

Scott retrieved the probe. The control came free. He shoved it quickly into the access hatch. "It's loose now. But there's no time. Press the button." Lights flared wildly around him as the probe sank deeper into its hole.

Spock was at Radha's station. The needle on her dial had climbed to warp fourteen point one. Uhura, looking across at him, said, "Magnetic force meter is steady, sir."

As she spoke, the needle on Radha's dial had sunk to warp thirteen. It continued to drop. Spock flipped the intercom. "Mr. Scott, you have accomplished your purpose."

Scott disengaged the magnetic probe. Then his head fell on the hot metal of the tube. "You might at least say thank you, Mr. Spock."

Spock was genuinely astounded. "For what purpose, Mr. Scott? What is it in you that requires an overwhelming display of emotion in a situation such as this? Two men pursue their only reasonable course— and you clearly seem to feel something more is necessary. What?"

"Never mind," Scott said wearily. "I'm sorry I brought it up."

The three stranded *Enterprise* men were nearing the big, red rock. And the readings on Sulu's tricorder still showed off the scale beyond their peak. Kirk approached the rock. "That closed door," he said, "must be right here."

They all shoved their shoulders against the rock. It didn't move. Panting, McCoy said, "If that's a closed door, it intends to stay closed."

The rock of itself slid to one side. It revealed a door that suddenly telescoped and drew upward. They stood in silence for a moment, peering inward.

"You think it's an invitation to go in?" McCoy said.

"If it is," Sulu said, "it's one that doesn't exactly relax me."

"The elevator door on the *Enterprise* bridge would be certainly preferable," Kirk agreed. "But whatever civilization exists on this planet is in there. And without the ship, gentlemen, in there is our sole source of food and water."

Following his lead, they cautiously moved through the doorway. It gave onto a large chamber. Athwart its entrance was a huge translucent cube. Pulsing in a thousand colors, lights flashed across its surfaces. "What is it?" Kirk said. "Does it house the brain that operates this place?" They were studying the cube when, between it and them, the woman appeared, wearing that same look of sadness. She moved toward them slowly.

"Tell us who you are for," Kirk said.

She didn't answer; but her arm rose and her pace increased.

"Form a circle," Kirk said. "Keep moving."

The woman halted. "You see," Kirk said, "you might as well tell us who you're for." He paused. "On the other hand, don't bother. You are still for Kirk."

"I am for James Kirk," she said.

McCoy and Sulu drew together in front of him as he said, "But James Kirk is not for you."

"Let me touch you—I beg it," she said. "It is my existence."

"It is my death," he said.

Her voice was very gentle. "I do not kill," she said.

"No? We have seen the results of your touch."

"But you are my match, James Kirk. I must touch you. Then I will live as your match even to the structure of your cells—the arrangement of chromosomes. I need you."

"That is how you kill. You will never reach me." Even as he spoke, he saw the second woman. Silently, unnoticed, she was moving toward them, arms outstretched. "Watch out!" he shouted.

"I am for McCoy," said the second woman.

Kirk jumped in front of Bones. "They are replicas!" he cried. "The computer there has programmed replicas!"

"They match our chromosome patterns after they touch us!" McCoy shouted.

A third woman, identical in beauty and clothing, slipped into view. "I am for Sulu," she said.

Aghast, the *Enterprise* men stared at each other. "Captain! We can no longer protect each other!"

McCoy said, "We could each make a rush at the other's killer!"

"It's worth a try," Kirk said.

Unhearing, dreamy, their arms extended, the trio of women were nearing them, closing in, closer and closer. Beside them, the air suddenly gathered into shimmer. Armed with phasers, Spock and an *Enterprise* security guard materialized swiftly. They swung their weapons around to cover the women.

"No, Spock!" Kirk yelled. "That cubed computer—destroy it!"

The phasers' beams struck the pulsing cube. There was a blast of iridescent light—and the women vanished. McCoy drew a great gasping sigh of incredulous relief. Kirk turned to Spock. "Mr. Spock, it is an understatement to say I am pleased to see you. I thought you and the *Enterprise* had been destroyed."

Spock holstered his phaser. "I had the same misgivings about you, Captain. We got back close enough to this planet to pick up your life form readings only a moment ago."

"Got back from where, Mr. Spock?"

But Spock was examining the broken cube with obvious admiration. "From where this brain had the power to send the ship . . . a thousand light years across the galaxy. What a magnificent culture this is."

"*Was*, Mr. Spock. Its defenses were run by computer."

Spock nodded. "I surmised that, Captain. Its moves were all immensely logical. But what people created it? Are there any representatives of them?"

"There were replicas of one of them. But now the power to reproduce them has been destroyed. Your phasers—" He stopped. On the blank wall of the chamber Losira's face was gradually forming. The lovely lips opened. "My fellow Kalandans, I greet you."

She went on. "A disease is decimating us. Beware of it. I regret giving you only this recorded warning— but we who have guarded this outpost for you may be dead by the time you hear it."

The voice faded. After a moment it resumed. "In creating this planet, we also created a deadly organism. I have awaited the regular supply ship from our home star with medical assistance, but I am now sickening with the virus myself. I shall set the outpost's controls on automatic. They will defend you against all enemies except the disease. My fellow Kalandans, I wish you well."

"She is wishing the dead well," McCoy said.

Spock had returned to the blasted computer. "It must have projected replicas of the only being available—Losira."

Kirk's eyes were on the dissolving image. "She was— beautiful," he said.

Spock shook his head. "Beauty is transitory, Captain. She was, however, loyal and highly intelligent."

The image on the wall had gone. Kirk opened his communicator. "Kirk to *Enterprise*. Five of us to beam up. By the way, Mr. Spock, I don't agree with you."

"Indeed, Captain?"

In Kirk's mind was the remembered sound of a

voice like music, of a dark and lonely loveliness waiting in vain for the salvation of her people. "Beauty survives, Mr. Spock. It survives in the memory of those who beheld it."

Spock stared at him. As they dematerialized, there was a sad little smile on Kirk's lips.

OBSESSION

(Art Wallace)

The ore was peculiar-looking, a harsh purple-black. Kirk struck it with a rock; but apart from its responsive clanging sound, it showed no trace of the blow. As he tossed the rock aside, he said, "Fantastic! It must be twenty times as hard as steel even in its raw state!"

Spock, his tricorder focused on the ore, said, "To be exact, Captain, 21.4 times as hard as the finest manganese steel."

Kirk opened his communicator. "Scotty? You can mark this vein of ore as confirmed. Inform Starfleet I recommend they dispatch a survey vessel to this planet immediately." As he spoke, a puff of white vapor drifted up over the rock matrix of the ore—a whisp of vapor hidden from the *Enterprise* men both by the rock's jutting and obscuring vegetation.

Scott said, "Acknowledged, Captain. They'll send a vessel fast enough for this rich a find."

Spock had pulled his phaser. "We won't be able to break it. I'll shoot off a sample."

Kirk didn't answer. He had stiffened abruptly, frowning, sniffing the air around him, his face strained like that of a man whose past had suddenly shouldered out his present. A shard of rock, grape-purple with the ore, had broken off; and the white vapor, as though guided by some protective intelligence, swiftly withdrew behind the big rock's shelter. As Spock rose from retrieving the ore sample, Kirk spoke. "Notice it?" he said. "A sweetish odor—a smell like honey? I wonder. It was years ago on a different planet . . . a 'thing' with an odor like that."

Some indefinable appeal in his voice moved Spock to say reassuringly, "This is the growing season in the hemisphere of this planet. There are doubtless many forms of pollen aromas around, Captain."

But Kirk was not soothed. He didn't seem to even have heard. Beckoning to the landing party's security officer, he said, "Lieutenant Rizzo, take two men and make a swing around our perimeter. Scan for any gaseous di-kironium in the atmosphere."

"Di-kironium," Spock observed, "does not exist except in laboratory experiments."

Kirk ignored the comment. "Set phasers on Disruptor-B. If you see any gaseous cloud, fire into it instantly. Make your sweep, Lieutenant."

A beep beeped from the open communicator in his hand; and Scott's voice said, "Ready to beam back aboard, sir?"

"Stand by, Scotty. We're checking something out."

"Sir, the U.S.S. *Yorktown* is expecting to rendezvous with us in less than eight hours. Doesn't leave us much time."

"Acknowledged. Continue standing by. Kirk out."

Spock, scanning the ore sample, spoke, his voice flat with awe. "Purity about eighty-five percent, Captain. With enough of this, they'll be building Starships with twice our warp capacity."

But Kirk was sniffing the air again. "Gone," he said. "It's gone now. I could have been wrong. The last time I caught that odor was about twelve years ago." He looked away to where the security officer and his men were quartering the area. Rizzo, standing near a small hillock, was bent over his tricorder. It had suddenly registered di-kironium on the air. Puzzling over it, he didn't see the cloud of white vapor encroaching on them from behind the hillock. "But that isn't possible," Rizzo muttered to himself. "Nothing can do that."

The vaporous cloud, however, seemed to obey laws

of its own. One moment it had been wispy, dia-
phonous; but in the next it had thickened to a dense
fog, moving suddenly and swiftly, emitting a humming
creature sound.

The scouting party whirled as one man. The coiling
colors that had appeared in the cloud reached out
a tentacle of green which touched the nearest security
man. He grabbed at his throat and fell to the ground.
As the second security man gagged, Rizzo pulled his
phaser. Where to direct his fire? Into the center of
the cloud? Where? He hesitated—and Kirk's communicator beeped.

"Captain . . . cloud," Rizzo choked. "A strange
cloud."

"Fire your phasers at its center!" Kirk shouted.

"Sir, we—help!"

"Spock, with me!" yelled Kirk. He raced toward the
hillock, his phaser drawn.

But the gaseous cloud was gone. Rizzo lay face down
on the grass, his communicator still clutched in his
hand. The bodies of his men lay near by. Kirk glanced
around before he hurried to Rizzo. The officer was
very pale. But where Rizzo's flesh was pale, the bodies
of his men were bone-white. Kirk lifted his head.
"Dead," he said. "And we'll find every red corpuscle
has been drained from their blood."

"At least Rizzo's alive," Spock said. "As you were
saying—you suspect what it was, Captain?"

Kirk had taken out his communicator. He nodded.
"A 'thing' . . . something that can't possibly exist. Yet
which *does exist*." He flipped the communicator open.
"Captain to *Enterprise*. Lock in on us, Scotty! Medical
emergency!"

He was in Sickbay. It didn't offer much room to
pace. So he stood still while Christine Chapel handed
the cartridge of tapes to Bones.

"The autopsy reports, Doctor."

"Thank you."

Kirk extended a hand to Christin'e arm. "Nurse, how
is Lieutenant Rizzo?"

"Still unconscious, Captain."

"Transfusions?" he said.

"Continuing as rapidly as possible, sir. Blood count still less than sixty percent of normal."

Kirk glanced at McCoy. But Bones was still deep in the autopsy reports. Kirk closed his eyes, running a hand over his forehead. Then he crossed to a communicator panel equipped with a small viewing screen.

"Kirk to bridge."

The voice was Spock's. "Ready to leave orbit, sir."

"Hold our position."

The image of Spock was supplanted by Scott's. "Cutting in, if I may, sir. The *Yorktown's* expecting to rendezvous with us in less than seven hours."

The heat of sudden rage engulfed Kirk. "Then inform them we may be late!"

McCoy turned from his desk. "Jim, the *Yorktown's* ship surgeon will want to know how late. The vaccines he's transfering to us are highly perishable."

Spock reappeared on the screen. "Sir, those medical supplies are badly needed on planet Theta Seven. They're expecting us to get them there on time."

I am hounded, Kirk thought. He looked from Spock back to McCoy. "Gentlemen," he said, "we are staying here in orbit until I learn more about those deaths. I am quite aware this may cost lives on planet Theta Seven. What lives are lost are my responsibility. Captain out." He switched off the screen, and addressed McCoy. "Autopsy findings?"

"You saw their color," McCoy said. "There wasn't a red corpuscle left in those bodies."

"Cuts? Incisions? Marks of any kind?"

"Not a one. What happened is medically impossible."

Kirk became conscious of a vast impatience with the human race. "I suggest," he said coldly, "that you check our record tapes for similar occurrences in the past before you speak of medical 'impossibilities'. I have in mind the experience of the U.S.S. *Farragut*. Twelve years ago it listed casualties from exactly the same impossible medical causes."

McCoy was eyeing him speculatively. "Thank you, Captain," he said tonelessly. "I'll check those tapes immediately."

"Yes, do," Kirk said. "But before you do, can you bring Lieutenant Rizzo back to consciousness for a moment?"

"Yes, I think so but—"

"Will it hurt him if you do?"

"In his condition it won't make much difference."

"Then bring him out of it," Kirk said. "I must ask him a question."

As they approached Rizzo's bed, Nurse Chapel was removing a small black box that had been strapped to his arm. "Transfusions completed, Doctor," she said. "Pulse and respiration still far from normal."

"Give him one cc. of cordrazine."

The nurse stared. Then picking up a hypodermic, she adjusted it. As it hissed against Rizzo's arm, Kirk's hands tightened on the bed bar until his knuckles whitened. On the pillow he saw the head move slightly. Kirk leaned in over Rizzo. "Lieutenant, this is the Captain. Can you hear me? Do you remember what happened to you?"

The eyelids fluttered. "Remember . . . I'm cold," Rizzo whispered. "So . . . cold."

Kirk pressed on. "Rizzo, you were attacked by something. When it happened, did you notice an odor of any kind?" His hands were shaking on the bed bar. He leaned in closer. "Rizzo, remember. A sickly sweet odor. Did you smell it?"

Horror filled the eyes. "Yes, sir . . . the smell . . . strange . . . like . . . like being smothered in honey."

Kirk exhaled a deep, quivering breath. "And—did you feel a—a *presence*? An intelligence?"

The head moved in assent. "It . . . it wanted strength from us. Yes, I felt it sucking. It was there."

McCoy moved in. "He's asleep. We can't risk another shot, Captain."

"He told me what I wanted to know."

"I wouldn't depend on his answers. In his half-conscious state, he could be dreaming, saying what he thought you wanted to hear."

Kirk straightened. "Check those record tapes, Doctor. I'll want your analysis of them as quickly as possible."

He left; Christine Chapel turned a puzzled face to McCoy. "What's the matter with the Captain, sir? I've never seen him like this."

"I intend to find out," McCoy said. "If I'm wanted, I'll be in the medical library."

On the bridge, Uhura greeted Kirk with a message from Starfleet. To her astonishment, he brushed it aside with a "Later, Lieutenant. Now have the security duty officer report to me here and at once." He crossed to Spock who said, "Continuing scanning, sir. Still no readings of life forms on the planet surface."

"Then, Mr. Spock, let's assume that it's something so totally different that our sensors would fail to identify it as a life form."

"You've mentioned—di-kironium, Captain."

"A rare element, Mr. Spock. Suppose a life form were composed of it, a strange, gaseous creature."

"There is no trace of di-kironium on the planet surface or in the atmosphere. I've scanned for the element, sir."

"Suppose it were able to camouflage itself?"

"Captain, if it were composed of di-kironium, lead, gold, hydrogen—whatever—our sensors would pinpoint it."

"Let's still assume I'm right."

"An illogical assumption, Captain. There is no way to camouflage a given chemical element from a sensor scan."

"No way? Let's further assume it's intelligent and knows we're looking for it."

"Captain, to hide from a sensor scan, it would have to be able to change its molecular structure."

Kirk stared at him. "Like gold changing itself to lead or wood to ivory. Mr. Spock, you've just suggested something which never occurred to me. And it answers

101

some questions in a tape record which I think you'll find Dr. McCoy is studying at this very moment."

Spock was on his feet. "Mr. Chekov! Take over on scanner." He was at the bridge elevator door as it hissed open to permit the entrance of the security duty officer. He was a new member of the crew, young, bright-faced, clearly dedicated as only the untried idealism of youth can dedicate itself. He strode to Kirk and saluted. "Ensign David Garrovick reporting, sir."

Kirk turned, startled. "You're the new security officer?"

"Yes, sir."

Kirk hesitated a moment. Then he said, "Was your father—?"

"Yes, sir. But I don't expect any special treatment on that account."

The shock in Kirk's face subsided. Now he snapped, "You'll get none aboard this ship, mister!"

"Yes, sir."

Uhura broke in. "I have a report on Lieutenant Rizzo, Captain. He's dead."

Kirk leaned back in his chair. It had been costly— the discovery of that so-precious purple ore. He turned back to the new security officer when he realized that Garrovick's face was grief-stricken, too.

"Did you know Rizzo?" Kirk said.

"Yes, sir. We were good friends. Graduated the Academy together."

Kirk nodded. "Want a crack at what killed him?"

"Yes, sir."

"Equip four men with phaser twos set for Disruptor effect. Report to the Transporter Room in five minutes. You will accompany me to the planet surface."

It was Garrovick who took the first tricorder reading of the terrain where the team materialized. Suddenly, he called to Kirk. "Sir, the reading is changing!"

Kirk crossed to him swiftly. Nodding, he examined the tricorder. "Spock was right," he said. "See—there's been a molecular shift."

"A di-kironium reading now, sir. Bearing is 94 mark 7, angle of elevation 6 degrees. Holding stationary."

Kirk pointed to a lift in the ground. "Behind that rise. Take two men and approach it from the right. I'll take two around the other way. As soon as you sight the creature, fire with full phasers. Remember—it's extremely dangerous."

Garrovick looked at the hill nervously. "Yes . . . sir." The words were spoken tightly. Kirk glanced at the tense young face. Then, turning, he said, "Swanson and Bardoli, come with me."

Garrovick and his two men had climbed the rise when he noticed that it fell to a deep gully. His men fanned out past the ravine. Garrovick stood still for a moment, staring down into it. Then, making his decision, he descended it, moving forward cautiously. Suddenly the white vapor gathered before him. Startled, taken off-guard by its foglike appearance, he stared at it, uncertain. Then he aimed his phaser and fired. The slice of its beam was a second too late. The cloud was gone.

Kirk yelled, "A phaser shot!" Racing toward the hill, he shouted, "Come on!"

He found Garrovick scrambling up the side of the gully, his eyes fixed on something ahead of him. "Garrovick, did you—?" He stopped short as he saw what Garrovick was crawling toward. The two men of his patrol lay motionless on the ground.

Kirk ran to the nearest one. When Garrovick joined him, his young face turned smeary with shock and misery. The features that stared up sightlessly from the ground were bone-white.

Kirk was alone in the Briefing Room. It felt good to be alone. Alone, it was easier to hold on to his conviction that the murderous creature which had killed five of his crewmen was the same one that had decimated the crew of the U.S.S. *Farragut* twelve years before in another quadrant of the galaxy. Five men. Sickbay had the unconscious survivor of Garrovick's team under treatment; but its transfusion had been unable to save the life of Rizzo. The thing was, he wasn't really alone. You never were. Always, you had the unspoken thoughts of other people to companion you. And he had the unspoken thoughts of Spock and McCoy to keep him company. Neither one credited the creature with its malignancy nor its intelligence. Moreover, they disapproved his decision to remain here and fight it to the death. And maybe they were right. Had he made a reliable command decision—or an emotional one?

He'd laid his forearms on the Briefing Room table. Now he lifted his head from them as Spock, followed by McCoy and Garrovick, entered. Spock and McCoy both gave him sharply appraising looks as they sat down. They tried to appear as though they hadn't— but they had. In his turn, Kirk tried to appear as though he hadn't noticed the looks.

He opened the session. "We've studied your report, Mr. Garrovick. I believe Mr. Spock has a question."

Spock said, "What was the size of the creature, Ensign?"

"I'd estimate it measured from ten to sixty cubic meters, sir. It changed size, fluctuated as it moved."

"Composition?"

"It was like a gaseous cloud, sir. Parts of it I could see through; other parts seemed more dense."

McCoy spoke. "Ensign, did you 'sense' any intelligence in this gaseous cloud?"

"Did I what, sir?"

"Did you get any subconscious impression that it *was* a creature? A living, thinking thing rather than just a strange cloud of chemical elements?"

"No, sir."

Kirk eyed Garrovick who twisted uncomfortably. "Ensign, you never came into actual contact with it, did you?"

"No, I didn't, sir. I was the furthest away." He paused. "It came out of nowhere, it seemed. It hovered a moment, then moved toward the nearest man. Fast, incredibly fast."

Kirk shoved a pencil on the table. "Did you say it hovered?"

"Yes, sir."

"You fired at it, didn't you?"

"Yes, sir."

"How close were you to the creature?"

"About twenty yards, sir."

"And you missed a hovering, large target at that distance?"

"Yes, sir. I . . . well, I didn't fire while it was hovering."

"Do you mean that you froze?"

"Not exactly, sir."

"Then tell us what you mean exactly."

"I was startled . . . maybe only for a second or so. And then by the time I fired, it—well, it was already moving."

Kirk's tone was curt. "Do you have any additional information for us?"

"No, sir. I only—hesitated for a second or so, sir. I'm sorry."

"Ensign, you're relieved of all duties and confined to your quarters until further notice."

Garrovick straightened. "Yes, sir."

McCoy's eyes followed him to the closing door. "You were a little hard on him, Jim."

"He froze. One of his men was killed. The other will probably die."

"Captain," Spock began.

Kirk rose. "You'll both be filing reports, gentlemen. Make your comments and recommendations then." He crossed briskly to the door. As he slammed it behind him, McCoy and Spock were left to stare at each other.

Garrovick's room was as dark as his discouragement. He found the light switch affixed to its panel with its labeled temperature gauges and other controls. Above the panel was an open-close switch marked "Ventilation Filter By-Pass." Garrovick, closing his eyes to all circumstances of his surroundings, gave himself up to his depression.

Back on the bridge, Kirk was greeted by another message from the *Yorktown* requesting information on the rendezvous. He ignored it; and Scott, approaching him, said, "While we wait, Captain, I've taken the liberty of cleaning the radioactive disposal vent on the number-two impulse engine. But we'll be ready to leave orbit in under half an hour."

"We're not leaving orbit, Engineer. Not that quickly."

Scott didn't take the hint. "The medicine for the Theta Seven colony is not only desperately needed, Captain, but has a limited stability. And—"

Kirk wheeled. "I am," he said, "familiar with the situation, Engineer. And I'm getting a little tired of my officers conspiring against me to force—" He broke off at the look on Scott's face. "Forgive me, Scotty. I shouldn't have used the word 'conspiring'."

"Agreed, sir."

Kirk strode over to Chekov. "Scanner readings?"

"Nothing, sir. Continuing to scan."

"Mr. Chekov, you're aware it may be able to change its composition? Are you scanning for any unusual movements? Any type of gaseous cloud?"

"We've run a full scanner probe twice, sir."

"Then do it twenty times if that's what it takes!"

He barked the words and left the bridge to his shocked personnel.

Garrovick wasn't the only victim of depression. Mc-Coy, viewing an autopsy tape, pulled it out of its slot, controlling an impulse to throw it to the floor. When Spock entered his office, he spoke no word of greeting.

"I hope I'm not disturbing you, Doctor."

"Interrupting another autopsy report is no disturbance, Spock. It's a relief."

"I need your advice," Spock said.

"Then I need a drink," said McCoy.

"I don't follow your reasoning, Doctor."

"You want advice from me? You must be kidding."

106

"I never joke. Perhaps I should rephrase my statement. I require an opinion. There are many aspects of human irrationality I do not yet comprehend. Obsession for one. The persistent, singleminded fixation on one idea."

"Jim and his creature?"

"Precisely. Have you studied the incident involving the U.S.S. *Farragut*?"

"With all these deaths and injuries, I've barely had time to scan them."

"Fortunately, I read fast," Spock said. "To summarize those records, I can inform you, Doctor, that almost half the crew, including the Captain, was annihilated. The Captain's name was Garrovick."

McCoy gave a startled whistle. "The same as our Ensign?"

"His father," Spock said. "I have the *Farragut* file here with me."

"Then there's more," McCoy said.

Spock nodded gravely. "A great deal more. Among the survivors of the disaster was a young officer on one of his first deep-space assignments." He nodded again at McCoy's look. "Yes, James T. Kirk," he said—and dropped the cartridge he held into the viewer. "And there's still more. I think you'd better study this record, Doctor."

Twenty minutes later McCoy sought the quarters of James T. Kirk, formerly of the U.S.S. *Farragut*. There was no response to the buzz at their door. McCoy opened it. "Mind if I come in, Jim?"

Kirk was lying on his bed, staring at the ceiling. He made no move. He spoke no word. Then, with a bound, he was off the bed to flip the switch on the wall communicator. "Kirk to bridge. Scanner report?"

Chekov's filtered voice said, "Continuing scanning, sir. No unusual readings."

"Maintain search. Kirk out." He turned from the communicator and jammed his right fist into his left hand. "It can't just vanish!" he cried.

"Sometimes they do if we're lucky." McCoy sat

107

down. "Monsters come in many forms, Jim. And know what's the greatest monster of them all? Guilt, known or unknown."

Kirk's jaw hardened. "Get to the point."

"Jim . . . a young officer exposed to unknown dangers for the first time is under tremendous emotional stress. We all know how—"

"Ensign Garrovick is a ship command decision, Doctor. You're straying out of your field."

"I was speaking," McCoy said, "of Lieutenant James T. Kirk of the Starship *Farragut*."

Kirk stared at him. He didn't speak, and McCoy went on. "Twelve years ago you were the young officer at the phaser station when something attacked your ship. According to the tape, this young officer insisted on blaming himself—"

"I delayed my fire at it!"

McCoy spoke sharply. "You had a normal, *human* emotion! *Surprise!* You were startled. You delayed firing for the grand total of perhaps two seconds!"

Kirk's face had grown drawn with remembered anguish. "If I hadn't delayed, the thing would have been destroyed!"

"The ship's exec didn't think so. His log entry is quite clear on the subject. He reported, 'Lieutenant Kirk is a fine officer who performed with uncommon bravery.'"

"I killed nearly two hundred men!"

McCoy's voice was very quiet. "Captain Garrovick was important to you, wasn't he?"

Kirk's shoulders slumped. He sank down on his bed, wringing his hands. "He was my commanding officer from the day I left the Academy. He was one of the finest men I ever knew." He leaped to his feet again. "I could have destroyed it! If I'd fired soon enough that first time . . ."

"*You don't know that, Jim!* You can't know it! Any more than you can know young Garrovick could have destroyed it."

Kirk's face was wiped clean of all emotions but torture. "I owe it to this ship . . ."

"To be so tormented by a memory . . . Jim, you can't destroy a boy because you see him as yourself as you were twelve years ago. You'll destroy yourself, your brilliant career."

"*I've got to kill this thing!* Don't ask me how I know that. I just know it."

McCoy eyed Kirk for a long moment. Then he rose and moved to the door, pressing the control that opened it. "Come in, Mr. Spock," he said.

Kirk whirled, crying, "Bones, don't push our friendship past the point that—"

McCoy interrupted. "This is professional, Captain. I am preparing a medical log entry on my estimate of the physical and emotional condition of a Starship's Captain. I require a witness of command rank."

Kirk's eyes swung from one of them to the other. Time—an infinity of it—went by. His voice when he spoke was edged with fury. "Do I understand, Doctor—and you, Commander Spock, that both or either of you believe me unfit or incapacitated?"

Spock said, "Correctly phrased as recommended in the manual, Captain. Our reply as also recommended is: we have noticed in your recent behavior items which, on the surface, seem unusual. We respectfully ask your permission to inquire further and—"

"Blast! Forget the manual!" Kirk shouted. "Ask your questions!"

Imperturbable, Spock said, "The U.S.S. *Yorktown* is now waiting for us at the appointed rendezvous, Captain. It carries perishable drugs which—"

Kirk ran a trembling hand over his forehead. "The news has a familiar ring, Commander."

McCoy said, "They need those vaccines on Theta Seven, Jim. Why are we delaying here?"

"Because I know what I know," Kirk said. "The creature that attacked the *Farragut* twelve years ago is the same—"

"Creature?" Spock said.

"Yes. My report was in the tape. As it attacked us twelve years ago, just as I lost consciousness, I could *feel* the intelligence of the thing; I could sense it thinking, planning."

"You say you could 'sense' its intelligence, Captain. How?" Spock said. "Did it communicate with you?"

McCoy broke in. "You state that it happened just as you lost consciousness. The semi-conscious mind is a tricky thing, Jim. A man can never be sure how much was real, how much was semi-conscious fancy."

"Real or unreal, Bones, it was deadly, lethal."

"No doubt of that," McCoy said.

"And if it *is* the same creature I met twelve years ago on a planet over a thousand light years from here?"

"Obviously, Captain, if it is an intelligent creature, if it is the same one, if therefore it is capable of space travel, it could pose a grave threat to inhabited planets."

"A lot of 'ifs,' Commander, I agree. But in my command judgment they still outweigh other factors. 'Intuition,' however illogical, Commander Spock, is recognized as a command prerogative."

"Jim, we're not trying to gang up on you."

"You haven't, Doctor. You've indicated a proper concern. You've both done your duty. May I be informed now of what medical log entry you intend to make?"

Spock and McCoy exchanged glances. "Jim," McCoy began.

Kirk smiled. "You've been bluffing, gentlemen. I'm calling your bluff."

Spock spoke. "This was totally my idea, Captain. Dr. McCoy's human affection for you makes him completely incapable of—"

McCoy interrupted. "*My affection* for him! I like that! Why, I practically had to sandbag you into this!" He turned to Kirk. "Jim, we were just using this to try and talk some sense into—"

The communicator beeped with the intercom signal. Chekov's excited voice said, "Bridge to Captain! Come in, Captain!"

Kirk was at the grill in a second flat. "Kirk here, Mr. Chekov."

"I have a reading on the—whatever it is, Captain! It's leaving the planet surface and heading into space!"

It was the measure of Kirk's nature that no triumph whatever colored the tone of his orders. "All decks, red alert! Prepare to leave orbit!"

Then he was gone out his door.

Gone out his door on a wild goose chase. Only what Kirk and the *Enterprise* chased through the labyrinths of trackless space was no wild goose. It was subtle as a cobra, swift as a mamba in its flight from the *Enterprise*, leading the Starship ever farther from its meeting with the *Yorktown* and its mission of mercy.

On the bridge they all knew what was at stake. The thing had twice changed its course in a malevolent, deliberate effort to mislead. Kirk was exhilarated past anxiety. But Scott was worried. "Captain, we can't maintain Warp 8 speed much longer. Pressures are approaching a critical point."

"Range, Mr. Chekov?" Kirk said.

"Point zero four light years ahead, sir. Our phasers won't reach it."

Spock spoke. "Captain, we're barely closing on it. We could be pursuing it for days."

"If necessary," Kirk said. He turned. "Do what you can to increase our speed, Mr. Scott."

"Aye, sir."

"Let's see it," Kirk said.

Chekov hit a button. "Magnification twelve, sir. There, sir! Got it on the screen!"

It was moving across the screen like an elongated comet, a coiling vortex floating amidst whirling vapors.

"How do you read it, Mr. Spock?"

"Conflicting data, sir. It seems to be in a borderline state between matter and energy. It can possibly utilize gravitational fields for propulsion."

"You don't find that sophisticated, Mr. Spock?"

"Extremely efficient, Captain." He paused. "Whether it indicates intelligence is another matter."

Chekov had got a red light on his console. "Open hatch on number-two impulse engine, sir. Mr. Scott was doing a clean-up job on it."

"Turn off the alarm," Kirk said. "We won't be using the impulse engines."

Scott turned from his station. "Captain! We can't do it! If we hold this speed, she'll blow up any minute!"

Kirk swallowed the pill of reality. "All right," he said. "Reduce to Warp Six."

In Garrovick's quarters the door buzzer sounded and Christine Chapel entered, carrying a dinner tray.

"Thank you," Garrovick said. "I'm not hungry."

"Dr. McCoy's orders."

"What's happening?" Garrovick said.

"Are we still chasing that thing half across the galaxy? Yes, we are. Has the Captain lost his sense of balance? Maybe. Is the crew about ready to explode? *Positively*. You're lucky to be out of it, Ensign."

Garrovick's voice was acid with bitterness. "Out of it? I *caused* it."

She calmly continued to spread food before him. "You know that's true, don't you?" he said. "If I'd fired my phaser quickly enough back on Argus Ten, none of this would have happened."

"Self-pity is a poor appetizer," she said. "Try the soup instead."

"I don't want it."

"If you don't eat," she told him, "Dr. McCoy will have you hauled down to Sickbay and make me feed you intravenously. I don't want to do that, either." Garrovick feebly returned her smile, nodded in defeat, and began to pick at his food. But it was no good. As the door closed behind her, a burst of frustration overwhelmed him. He dashed a cup of coffee he'd just poured against the wall. It hit the panel. Shattering against the switch of the ventilation filter by-pass, it knocked it to the open position.

At the same moment the strident alarm signal sounded. Kirk's voice came over the communicator.

"Battle stations! All decks to battle stations! The enemy is reducing speed! This is not a drill! All decks to battle stations!"

On the bridge Chekov shouted. "It's coming to a full halt, Captain! Magnification one, visual contact!"

Centered on the screen, now only a small object, the strange creature seemed to be pulsating. Kirk said, "Hello, Beautiful." Then he leaned toward Chekov. "Move in closer, Mr. Chekov. Sublight, one quarter speed."

As Chekov manipulated his controls, the bridge elevator door opened; and Garrovick, his face pale with tension, emerged to cross quickly over to Kirk. "Sir, request permission to return to my post."

"Within phaser range now, sir!" cried Chekov.

"Lock phasers on target, Mr. Chekov!"

"Locked on target, sir!"

"Fire main phasers!"

But the fierce energy blips passed directly through the creature. Stunned, Kirk watched in unbelief.

"Phasers ineffectual, Captain!"

"Photon torpedoes, Mr. Chekov! Minimum spread pattern!"

"Minimum pattern ready, sir!"

"Fire!"

The ship lurched slightly. The target emitted a flash of blinding light and the *Enterprise* rocked. Uhura cried, "There—on the screen! It's still coming toward us, sir!"

The vaporous creature was growing larger, denser on the screen. "Deflectors up!" Kirk ordered.

"Deflectors up, sir."

Spock spoke into the awed silence. "The deflectors will not stop it, Captain." He was stooping, intent on his hooded viewer. "I should have guessed this! For the creature to be able to use gravity as a propulsive force, it would have to possess the capacity to flow through our deflector screens!"

"Any way to stop it, Mr. Spock?"

"Negative, Captain. It is able to throw its particles

113

slightly out of time synchronization. It seems to measure our force-field pulsations—and stays a split second in front or behind them."

Chekov said, "Contact in five seconds, sir!"

Kirk hit his intercom button. "All decks, all stations, intruder alert!"

"All vents and hatches secure, sir," Chekov said. "All lights on the board show green—*No! Sir, the number-two impulse hatch! We've got a red light on it!*

Kirk whirled toward the screen. The cloudlike thing was on the ship now. Suddenly, it disappeared.

Scott turned, crying, "Captain! Something has entered through the number-two impulse vent!"

"Negative pressure all ship's vents! Mr. Chekov alert all decks!"

Red lights flashed to the ear-splitting howl of the alarm sirens.

"Well? Reports?"

Though Spock and McCoy sat at the Briefing Room table, it was Scott to whom the questions were directed. He knew it and looked away from Kirk's accusing eyes. "Sir, when it entered through impulse engine-two vent, it attacked two crewmen there before it went into the ventilation system."

"Bones?" Kirk said.

"One man has a bare chance of survival. The other is dead. So you can hang that little price tag to your monster hunt!"

"That's enough, Bones."

"It's *not* enough! You didn't care what happened as long as you could hang your trophy on the wall! Well, it's not *on* the wall, Captain! It's *in* it!"

Scott added his drop of reality to Kirk's cup of self-castigation. "With the ventilation system cut off, sir, we've air for only two hours."

Human beings with a cause, Kirk thought. You must not look to them for mercy. As though to confirm the thought, McCoy said, "I expect things don't look much brighter to the patients on colony Theta Seven."

114

Only in Spock, the half human, was there mercy. "May I suggest that we no longer belabor the point of whether or not we should have pursued the creature? The matter has become academic. The creature is now pursuing *us.*"

"Creature, Mr. Spock?" said McCoy.

"*It turned and attacked, Doctor.* Its method was well considered and intelligent."

Kirk spoke very slowly. "I have no joy in being proved right, gentlemen, believe me. It could have been many light years away from us by now. But, instead, it chose to stop here. Why? Why? Why?"

"I must wait, Captain," Spock said. "Until I can make a closer analysis of the creature."

"We have two hours, Mr. Spock." Kirk turned to Scott. "Try flushing your radioactive waste into the ventilator system. It might cause some discomfort."

"Aye, sir."

McCoy rose with him. He halted at the door. "Jim, sorry about that few minutes ago. Your decision to go after it was right."

The exoneration should have meant something. It didn't. If you weren't companioned by the condemning thoughts of other people, you were companioned by those of your own conscience. Spock spoke. "Captain," he said, "the creature's ability to throw itself out of time, to desynchronize, allows it to be elsewhere in the instant our phasers strike. There is no basis, then, for your self-recrimination. If you had fired your phaser precisely on time twelve years ago, it would have made no more difference than it did an hour ago. Captain Garrovick would still be dead."

"Theories of guilt, of right or wrong, past and present—I seem to have outgrown them suddenly. Suddenly, Mr. Spock, my sole concern is saving my ship and my crew."

"The fault was not yours, Captain. There was no fault."

Kirk rose. "If you want to play psychoanalyst—and frankly, it's not your role, Spock—do it with Ensign

Garrovick. Not me. Thank you." He left the Briefing Room without a backward glance.

Spock took the hint. He buzzed the door of Garrovick's quarters and walked in. Garrovick leaped to his feet.

"You may be seated, Ensign. I wish to talk to you." The young face was puzzled. "Yes, sir."

"Ensign, am I correct in my assumption that you have been disturbed by what you consider a failure to behave in the prescribed manner in a moment of stress?"

Garrovick flushed painfully. "Well, I haven't been exactly proud of myself, sir."

"Perhaps you have considered this so-called failure of yours only from the standpoint of your own emotions."

Garrovick shook his head. "No, sir. I've considered the facts, too. And the facts are that men under my command died because I hesitated, because I stopped to analyze instead of acting. My attempt to be logical killed my men, Mr. Spock."

"Ensign, self-intolerance is an hereditary trait of your species."

"You make it sound like a disease, sir."

Their eyes, fixed on each other, failed to note the slight wisp of vapor that was filtering out of the jammed ventilator opening. Garrovick made a gesture of impatience. "You're telling me, 'Don't worry about it, Ensign! It happens to all of us. We'll just bury the bodies and won't think about them any more.' Isn't that it, Mr. Spock?"

"Not quite. You can learn from remorse, Ensign. It changes the human constitution. But guilt is a waste of time. Hate of the self, always undeserved, will ultimately crush you."

Spock paused suddenly, sniffing the air. "Do you smell anything?" he asked. "I thought I scented—" Then he saw the trail of mist drifting from the ventilator.

Garrovick whirled toward it. "Sir, it's the . . ."

Spock, grabbing his arm, propelled him to the door. "Out of here—fast! I will attempt to seal it off!"

He rushed to the ventilator opening. Seizing the jammed switch, he struggled to close it. But the cloud, full and dense now, was pouring into the room, over him, around him, and finally completely obscuring him.

In the corridor Garrovick raced to a wall communicator. "Captain! The creature! It's in my cabin, sir! It's got Mr. Spock!"

Kirk leaped from his chair. "On my way, Garrovick!" He dropped his speaker. "Scotty, reverse pressure, Cabin 341! Lieutenant Uhura, Security to 341! Medical alert!"

He'd given the right orders. In Garrovick's quarters, the creature, pulled by the suction of reversed pressure, was drawn back into the ventilator opening. McCoy, with a Security team, met him outside the door. As McCoy reached to open it, Kirk said, "Wait, Bones! We need a tricorder reading!"

As a guard adjusted his instrument, McCoy cried out, "Jim, Spock may be dying!"

Kirk whirled. "If we release that thing into the ship, he'll have a lot of company!"

Garrovick, ashen, spoke. "It's my fault, sir. I must have jammed the vent control when I hit a cup against it."

Kirk spoke to the guard. "Check if the reverse pressure has pulled it back into the ventilation system!"

"He saved my life, sir," Garrovick said brokenly. "I should be lying dead in there, not him."

Spock's voice came through the door. "I am gratified that neither of us is dead, Ensign." He flung the door open. "The reverse pressure worked, Captain. The vent is closed."

Stunned, Kirk stared at him. "Spock, don't misunderstand my question—but why aren't you dead?"

"That green blood of his!" shouted McCoy.

Spock nodded. "My hemoglobin is based on copper, not iron."

Kirk had moved to the cabin door, sniffing at it. "The scent—it's different. Yes . . . Yes, I think I understand now."

"You don't really believe you're in communication with the creature, Captain?"

"I'm not sure what it is, Spock. But you remember I said I knew it was alive. Perhaps it's not communication as we understand it, but I did know it was alive and intelligent. Now I know something else."

The wall communicator beeped. "Bridge to Captain Kirk."

Kirk flipped the switch. "Kirk here."

"Scott, sir. The creature's moving back toward the number-two impulse vent. The radioactive flushing may be affecting it."

"Open the vent," Kirk said. "On my way. Kirk out." He was running down the corridor when he hesitated and turned back. "Ensign Garrovick!"

Garrovick hastened to him. "Yes, sir?"

"You were on the bridge when we were attacked."

"I'm sorry, sir. I know I'd been confined to quarters, but when the alert sounded for battle stations, I . . ."

"Very commendable, Ensign. What was your impression of the battle?"

"I don't understand, sir."

"I'm asking for your military appraisal of the techniques employed against the creature."

Garrovick's jaw firmed. "Ineffective, sir." He added hastily. "I mean, Captain, you did everything possible. It's just that nothing works against a monster that can do what that thing does."

"And what's your appraisal of your conduct back on the planet?"

"I delayed firing."

"And if you had fired on time?" Kirk waited, his eyes on Garrovick's eyes. "It would have made no difference, Ensign. No weapon known would have made any difference. Then—or twelve years ago."

"Pardon, sir? I don't understand."

"I said, return to duty, Mr. Garrovick."

Joy flooded the young face. "Yes, sir. Thank you, Captain."

He was about to add something, but the elevator doors had already closed on Kirk.

There was news awaiting him on the bridge. Chekov, moving aside to surrender Spock's station to him, spoke eagerly. "Results positive, Captain. The creature has left the ship at high warp speed and is already out of scanner range."

Kirk had joined Spock at his station. "Direction, Mr. Spock?"

"Bearing was 127, mark 9. But I've already lost it now, sir."

Kirk switched on the intercom. "Scotty. I'm going to want all the speed you can deliver. Stick with it until we begin to shake apart. Kirk out." He turned to Spock. "I believe I know where it's going."

"It has changed course before to mislead us, sir. Logic would dictate that—"

"I'm playing intuition instead of logic, Mr. Spock. Mr. Chekov, compute a course for the Tychos Star System."

Heads snapped around. Controlling his surprise, Chekov punched in the course. "Computed and on the board, sir."

"Ahead full."

"Ahead full, sir."

"Lieutenant Uhura, contact the U.S.S. *Yorktown* and Starfleet. Inform both that we're pursuing the creature to planet 4 of that System. It's the location of its attack on the U.S.S. *Farragut* twelve years ago."

Spock said, "I don't understand, Captain."

"Remember when I said that the scent of the creature was somehow different? Something in my mind then said, 'birth . . . divide . . . multiply.' It said 'home'."

Spock's eyebrows went up. "And you know where 'home' is, Captain?"

"Yes. Home is where it fought a Starship once before. Lieutenant Uhura, give them our tactical situation. Tell them that I am committing this vessel to the creature's destruction. We will rendezvous with the *Yorktown*—" He turned to Chekov. "Round trip, Mr. Chekov?"

"One point seven days, sir."

"Lieutenant Uhura, we will rendezvous with the *Yorktown* in forty-eight hours."

Planet 4 of the Tychos Star System was a strangely dull, lifeless-looking one. On the bridge McCoy eyed its viewer image with distaste. He spoke to Spock. "I assume you also think we should pursue this creature and destroy it."

"Definitely, Doctor."

"You don't agree with us, Bones?"

McCoy shrugged. "It's a mother. I don't happen to enjoy destroying mothers."

Spock said, "If the creature is about to spawn, it will undoubtedly reproduce by fission, not just in two parts but thousands."

Kirk glanced at him. "Anti-matter seems to be our only possibility then."

Spock nodded. "An ounce should be sufficient. We can drain it out of our engines, transport it to the planet in a magnetic vacuum field."

Garrovick had taken up a position beside Kirk's chair. "Ensign, contact medical stores. I want as much hemoplasm as they can spare. And I want it in the Transporter Room in fifteen minutes."

"Yes, sir."

"You intend to use the hemoplasm to attract the creature?" McCoy asked.

"We have to lure it to the anti-matter. As it's attracted by red blood cells, what better bait can we have?"

"There remains one problem, Captain."

Kirk nodded at Spock. "The blast."

"Exactly. A matter-anti-matter blast will rip half the planet's atmosphere away. If our ship is still in orbit, and encounters those—shock waves . . ."

'We'll have to take that chance."

Spock said, "No one can guarantee our Transporter will operate under such conditions. If a man is beaming up when that blast hits, we may lose him, Captain."

Garrovick who had returned was listening intently. He flushed as Kirk said, "That's why I've decided to set the trap myself, Mr. Spock."

Spock got up. "Captain, I have so little hemoglobin in my blood the creature would not be able to harm me extensively. It would seem logical for me to be the one who—"

"Negative, Mr. Spock. I want you on board in case this fails. In that case another plan will have to be devised."

"Captain," Spock persisted, "it will require two men to transport the anti-matter unit."

"Sir," Garrovick said. "Sir, I request permission to go with you."

Kirk regarded him speculatively. Then he nodded. "Yes," he said. "I had you in mind, Mr. Garrovick."

Desolation—a brittle world of death was the world of the creature, its surface scarred and blackened by lava fissures, the hideous corrugations of dead volcanoes. As they materialized on it, Kirk and Garrovick staggered under the burden of the anti-matter unit, their anti-gravs tight on the brilliant metal sphere suspended between them. The hemoplasm container took form beside them. The moment he found secure footage on his lava ridge, Kirk freed a hand to open his communicator.

"Kirk to *Enterprise*."

"Spock here, Captain."

"Proceed immediately to maximum distant orbit, Mr. Spock."

"Yes, sir."

Garrovick said, "this is the ultimate, sir. Less than an ounce of anti-matter here . . . and yet more power than ten thousand cobalt bombs."

Kirk nodded. "A pound of it would destroy a whole solar system. I hope it's as powerful as man is allowed to get."

121

There was a small rise in front of them. Leaving the hemoplasm where it lay, they carefully positioned the anti-matter container on the little hillock of flattened lava.

"Detonator," Kirk said.

Garrovick handed him a small device. Moving with utmost care, Kirk attached it to the container. Then, with the flick of a switch, he armed it. That done, he reopened his communicator.

"Kirk to *Enterprise*."

"Spock here, Captain. Holding at thirty thousand kilometers."

"Anti-matter container positioned and armed. I'll call back when I've baited it. Kirk out."

"Captain! Look!"

The vaporous thing had fully emerged from a lava fissure and was flowing over the hemoplasm, ingesting it. "The hemoplasm!" Garrovick cried. "The bait's already gone!"

Kirk straightened. "We'll have to use something else."

"But it only feeds on blood!"

Kirk's older eyes met the younger ones. "Transport back to the ship, Ensign. Tell them to prepare to detonate."

Garrovick was aghast. "You, sir? *You're* going to be the bait?"

"You heard your order. Get back to the ship!"

Garrovick didn't respond. He looked again toward the creature. Gorged on the hemoplasm, it was still hovering over the container. Then, very slowly, it began to move toward the two humans.

Kirk grabbed Garrovick's arm, and swung him around. "I gave you an order!" he shouted.

"Yes, sir." He took out his communicator; and starting to walk slowly past Kirk, prepared to give beam-up instructions. Then, without warning, he whirled and struck Kirk with a sharp karate chop on the back of the neck. Kirk fell. Garrovick, glancing quickly toward the creature, stooped to pick up Kirk's body. Kirk lashed out with a kick that threw Garrovick off-balance. He stumbled and Kirk jumped to his feet.

"Ensign, consider yourself on report! We don't have time in this service for heroics. I have no intention of sacrificing myself. Come on!" He yanked Garrovick into a position that placed the anti-matter unit between them and the creature. Then he opened his communicator. "Kirk to *Enterprise*!"

"Spock, Captain."

"Scan us, Spock and lock onto us. It's going to be very close. Stand by." He looked back. The creature was almost on him, a thin tentacle of mist drifting toward his throat.

"I—I can smell it, Captain. It's sickly . . . honey sweet."

"Stand by, *Enterprise*," Kirk said. He saw that the creature, seeking blood in the anti-matter unit, was flowing over the metal sphere. Shouting into his communicator, he cried, *"Now Energize! And detonate!"*

Their bodies went into shimmer, fading. Then the world of the creature blew up.

In the Transporter Room of the *Enterprise*, Spock saw the forms of Kirk and Garrovick begin to take shape. They held it only for a fleeting second before they dissolved once more into shining fragments. Spock's steady hands worked at the controls, adjusting them. Scott, panic-stricken, flung himself at the Transporter console. McCoy yelled, "Don't just stand there! For God's sake, *do* something!"

Chekov spoke over the intercom. "All decks, stand by. Shock waves!"

The Transporter Room rocked crazily. Spock and Scott, flung to their knees, struggled desperately to stay with the console controls. Then they both looked over at the Transporter chamber. It was empty.

Spock said, "Cross-circuit to B, Mr. Scott."

McCoy uttered a literal howl. *"What a crazy way to travel! Spilling a man's molecules all over the damned universe!*

Scott said, "Picking it up . . . I think we're picking them up."

McCoy looked away from the empty Transporter chamber. When he found what it took to look back, two forms were again assuming shape and substance. Kirk and Garrovick stepped from the platform—whole, unharmed.

Scott sank down over the console. "Captain," he said as though to himself. "Captain." He sighed. "Thank God."

Spock was reproving. "There was no deity involved, Mr. Scott. It was my cross-circuit to selector B that recovered them."

McCoy eyed Spock with disgust. "Well, thank pitchforks and pointed ears, then! As long as they worked!"

Kirk used his communicator. "Captain Kirk to bridge."

"Chekov here, Captain."

"Lay a course for the *Yorktown* rendezvous, Mr. Chekov. Maximum warp."

"Aye, sir."

Kirk smiled at Garrovick. "Come to my cabin when you've cleaned up, Ensign. I want to tell you about your father. Several stories I think you'll like to hear."

Garrovick looked at him, adoration in his eyes.

"Thank you, sir. I will."

THE RETURN OF THE ARCHONS

(Boris Sobelman)

Once it had been a hundred years before—that time past when the Starship *Archon* had been lost to mysterious circumstances on the planet Beta 3000.

Now it was time present; and the two crewmen from another Starship, the *Enterprise*, down on the same planet scouting for news of the *Archon*, seemed about to list themselves as "missing," too. They were running swiftly down a drab street of an apparently innocuous town of the apparently innocuous planet when one of them stumbled and fell. Sulu, his companion, paused, reaching down a muscular hand. "O'Neill, get up! We've got to keep going!"

Nobody on the street turned to look at them. Nobody offered to help them. If ever there were passersby, the inhabitants of Beta 3000 could qualify for the "I don't care" prize. Still prone on the street, Lieutenant O'Neill was panting. "It's no use, Mr. Sulu. They're everywhere! Look! There's one of them—there's one of the Lawgivers!" He gestured toward a hooded creature who was approaching, a staff in its hand. Then he pointed to a second figure, similarly hooded, robed and staved. "They're everywhere! We can't get away from them!"

Sulu opened his communicator. "Scouting party to *Enterprise!* Captain, beam us up! Quick! Emergency!" He looked down at O'Neill. "Just hold on, Lieutenant. They'll beam us back to the ship any minute now—"

But O'Neill had scrambled wildly to his feet. "Run,

125

I tell you! We've got to get away! You know what they're capable of!"

"O'Neill—"

But the Lieutenant was racing down the street. Sulu, distracted, his eyes on the flying figure of O'Neill, was scarcely aware that the nearest hooded being had lightly touched him with its staff. He was conscious only of a sudden sense of peace, of the tension in him ebbing, giving way to an inflow of a beatific feeling of unmarred tranquility. He was not permitted to enjoy it for long. The *Enterprise*'s Transporter had fixed on him —and he was shimmering into dematerialization.

But completing his transportation wasn't easily accomplished. On the *Enterprise* the Transporter's console lights flicked on, dimmed, flicked off, brightened again. Kirk, with Scott and young sociologist Lindstrom, watched them. When Sulu's figure finally collected form and substance, he was astonished to see it clad, not in its uniform, but in the shaggy homespun of the shapeless trousers and sweater that was the customary male apparel of Beta 3000's citizenry. He hurried forward. "Sulu, what's happened? Where's Lieutenant O'Neill?"

Sulu's answer was dull as though something had thickened his tongue. "You . . . you are not of the Body."

Kirk glanced at Scott. The engineer nodded. Speaking into his mike, he said, "Dr. McCoy . . . Transporter Room, please. And quickly."

It was with most delicate care and deliberation that Sulu stepped from the Transporter platform. He looked at Lindstrom and his face was suddenly convulsed with fury. He lifted the bundled uniform he held under an arm—and lifting it up, he shook it furiously at Lindstrom. "You did it!" he shouted. "They knew we were Archons! These are the clothes Archons wear! Not these, not these—" he gestured to his own rough clothing. Then he hurled the uniform at Lindstrom.

Kirk said, "Easy, Sulu. It's all right. Now tell me what happened down there."

Sulu staggered. As Kirk extended a hand to steady him, McCoy hurried in, medical kit in hand. He halted to stare. "Jim! Where's O'Neill?"

Kirk shook his head for answer; and Sulu, tensing as though to receive a message of immense significance, muttered "Landru . . . Landru . . ."

The sheer meaninglessness of the mutter chilled Kirk. "Sulu, what happened down there? What did they do to you?"

The answer came tonelessly. "They're wonderful," Sulu said. "The sweetest, friendliest people in the universe. They live in paradise, Captain."

Nor in Sickbay could McCoy elicit anything from Sulu but the same words, the same phrases over and over. He talked gramophonically, like a record damned to endlessly repeat itself. It was this repetitiousness added to his inability to account either for his own condition or O'Neill's disappearance that decided Kirk to beam down to the planet with an additional search detail. When they materialized—Kirk, Spock, McCoy, Lindstrom, and two security crewmen—it was alongside a house, a brick house that bordered on an alley facing a wide street.

"Materialization completed," Kirk said into his communicator. "Kirk out." As he snapped it shut, he saw that Lindstrom had already edged out into the street and was examining it, his young face alight with interest and curiosity. They followed him—and at once, among the passing people, Kirk noted two hooded beings, cowled and in monkish robes who carried long stafflike devices. What could be seen of their faces was stony, as though any expression might divulge some secret of incalculable value. Their eyes looked dead— filmed and unseeing. One of the people, a man, shambled toward them. His smile was as vacuous as it was amiable; but Kirk took care to return his nod.

As he moved on, Spock said, "Odd."

"Comment, Mr. Spock?"

"That man's expression, Captain. Extremely similar to that of Mr. Sulu when we beamed him up from here. Dazed, a kind of mindlessness."

"Let's find out if all the planet's inhabitants are like him," Kirk said. He walked boldly out into the street, followed by his group. Each of the passers-by they met greeted them with the same bland smile. Then a young, biggish man with an empty, ingenuous face stopped to speak to Kirk. "Evenin', friend. Mah name's Bilar. What's yourn?"

"Kirk."

He got the stupid smile. "You-all be strangers."

Kirk nodded and Bilar said, "Here for the festival, ayeh? Got a place to sleep it off yet?"

"No. Not yet," Kirk said.

"Go round to Reger's house. He's got rooms." The oafish face glanced down the street at the clock in the tower of what might have been the Town Hall. "But you'll have to hurry. It's almost the Red Hour."

The shorter hand of the clock was close to the numeral six. "This festival," Kirk said, "it starts at six?"

But Bilar's interest had been distracted by a pretty girl, dark and slim, who was hurrying toward them. He put out a hand to stop her. "Tula, these here folks be strangers come for the festival. Your daddy can put them up, can't he?"

Tula, her dark eyes on Lindstrom's handsome blondness, smiled shyly. "You're from over the valley?" she asked.

Lindstrom smiled back at her. "That's right. We just got in."

"Don't see valley folks much. My father'll be glad to take you in. He don't care where folks come from."

"He runs a rooming house?" Kirk said.

She laughed. "That's a funny name for it. It's right over there." She pointed to a comfortable-looking, three-story structure down the street—and at the same moment the tower clock struck the first stroke of six. A scream, strident, sounding half-mad, broke from the respectable-faced matron near by. A man, a foot or so away from Kirk, suddenly lunged at him. Kirk elbowed the blow aside, hurling him back, and cried to his men, "Back to back!" They closed together in the defensive movement. Then pandemonium, apparently causeless, burst out around them. Men were grimly embattled, battering at each other with bare fists, stones, clubs. A fleeing woman, shrieking, was pursued across the street by a man, intent, silent, exultant. From somewhere came the crashing sounds of smashing windows. Then, to their horror, Tula, twisting and writhing, opened her mouth to a high ecstatic screaming. Bilar rushed at her, shouting, "Tula, Tula! Come!" He seized her wrist, and as Lindstrom leaped forward to grapple with him, stooped for a stone on the street. He crashed it down on Lindstrom's shoulders, felling him. McCoy, hauling the sociologist back to his feet, cried, "Jim, this is madness!"

"Madness doesn't hit an entire community at once, Bones—" Kirk broke off, for rocks had begun to fall among them. One of their attackers, aiming a thick club at him, yelled "Festival! Festival! Festival!" Froth had gathered on the man's lips and Kirk said, "Let's go! That house—where the girl was taking us!—make for it!"

Bunched together, they moved down the street; a young woman, beautiful, her dress torn, grabbed Kirk's arm, pulling at it to drag him off. He shook her loose and she ran off, shrieking with wild, maniacal laughter. More rocks struck them and Kirk, wiping a trickle of blood from a cut on his cheek, shouted, "Run!"

The bedlam pursued them to the door of the house. Kirk hammered on it. And after a moment it was opened. Kirk slammed it closed behind them; one of the three elderly men who confronted him stared at him in astonishment. "Yes?"

"Sorry to break in like this," Kirk said. "We didn't expect the kind of welcome we received."

One of the other men spoke. "Welcome? You are strangers?"

"Yes," Kirk said. "We're . . . from the valley."

The third man said, "Come for the festival?"

"That's right," Kirk told him.

"Then how come you here?"

Kirk adressed the first man who had greeted them. "Are you Reger?"

"I am.'

"You have a daughter named Tula?"

"Yes."

Lindstrom burst into speech. "Well, you'd better do something about her! She's out there alone in that madness!"

Reger averted his eyes. "It is the festival," he said. "The will of Landru . . ."

The third man spoke again. "Reger, these are young men! They are not old enough to be excused!"

"They are visitors from the valley, Hacom," Reger said.

In the wrinkled sockets of Hacom's eyes shone a sudden, fanatic gleam. "Have they no Lawgivers in the valley? Why are they not with the festival?"

Kirk interposing, said, "We heard you might have rooms for us, Reger."

"There, Hacom, you see. They seek only a place to rest after the festival."

"The Red Hour has just begun!" Hacom said.

The tone was so hostile that Reger shrank. "Hacom, these be strangers. The valley has different ways."

"Do you say that Landru is not everywhere?"

The second man tried to assume the role of peacemaker. "No, of course Reger does not blaspheme. He simply said the valley had different ways."

Reger had recovered himself. "These strangers have come to me for lodging. Shall I turn them away?" Then, speaking directly to Kirk, he said, "Come, please . . ."

"But Tula, the girl!" Lindstrom cried. "She's still out there!"

Hacom eyed him with openly inimical suspicion. "She is in the festival, young sir. As you should be."

Uneasy, Reger said, "Quickly, please. Come."

Kirk, turning to follow, saw Hacom turn to the second man. "Tamar, the Lawgivers should know about this!"

Tamar's reply was gently equivocal. "Surely, Hacom, they already know," he said. "Are they not infallible?"

But Hacom was not to be appeased. "You mock

130

them!" he cried. "You mock the Lawgivers! And these strangers are not of the Body!" He strode to the street door, flung it open—crying, "You will see!"—and disappeared.

His departure did not dismay Kirk. They were on the right trail. Incoherent though they were, the references to "Landru," to membership in some vague corpus, corporation, brotherhood, or society they termed the "Body" matched the ravings of Sulu on his return to the *Enterprise*. He was content with the progress they'd made, though the room they were shown into was bare except for a dozen or so thin pallets scattered about its floor. From the open window came the screamings and howlings of the riotous festival and its celebrations. Reger spoke tentatively to Kirk. "Sir, you can return here at the close of the festival. It will be quiet. You will have need of rest."

"Reger," Kirk said, "we have no plans to attend the festival."

The news shook his host. He went to the window and lifted it more widely open to the unroarious hullabaloo outside. "But the hour has struck!" he cried. "You can hear!"

"What I'd like to hear is more about this—festival of yours," Kirk said. "And about Landru I'd like to hear."

Reger cringed at the word "Landru". He slammed down the window. "Landru," he whispered. "You ask me . . . you are strange here . . . you scorn the festival. Are you—who are you?"

"Who is Landru?" Kirk said.

Reger stared, appalled, at him. Then, wheeling, he almost ran from the room. Lindstrom made a move to reopen the window and Kirk said, "Leave it shut, Mr. Lindstrom."

"Captain, I'm a sociologist! Don't you realize what's happening out there?"

"Our mission," Kirk said evenly, "is to find out what happened to the missing Starship *Archon* and to our own Lieutenant O'Neill. We are not here to become involved with—"

Lindstrom interrupted excitedly. "But it's a bacchanal! And it occurred spontaneously to these people at one and the same time! I've got to know more about it—find out more!"

Kirk's voice had hardened. "Mr. Lindstrom, you heard me! This is not an expedition to study the folkways of Beta 3000!"

Spock broke in. "Captain, in view of what's happening outside, may I suggest a check on Mr. Sulu's condition? What were his reactions . . . if any—at the stroke of six o'clock?"

Kirk nodded. "Thank you, Mr. Spock." He flipped open his communicator to say, "Kirk here. Lieutenant Uhura, report on Mr. Sulu."

"I think he's all right now, sir. How did you know?"

"Know what, Lieutenant?"

"That he'd sort of run amuck. They're putting him under sedation, sir."

"How long ago did he run amuck? Exactly?"

"Six minutes, Captain."

"Did he say anything?"

"Nothing that made any sense, sir. He kept yelling about Landru, whatever that is. Is everything all right down there, Captain?"

"So far. Keep your channels open. Kirk out."

"Landru," he said reflectively—and moved to the window. The street scene it showed was not reassuring. To the left two men flailed at each other with hatchet-shaped weapons. Another, chasing a shrieking, half-naked woman across the street, vanished, shouting, around a corner. Bodies were scattered, prone in the dust of the street. A short distance down it a building was aflame; among the people still milling about before Reger's house, riots erupted unchecked, then subsided only to break out again. A big bonfire blazed in the street's center.

Kirk turned away to re-face his men. "My guess is we have until morning. Let's put the time to good use. Bones, we need atmospheric readings to determine if something in the air accounts for this. Lindstrom, correlate what you've seen with other sociological parallels, if any. Mr. Spock, you and I have some

132

serious thinking to do. When we leave here in the morning, I want to have a plan of action."

The night did not vouchsafe much sleep. But the twelve noisy hours that moved the tower clock's small hand to the morning's sixth hour finally passed; at the first stroke of its bell, absolute silence fell upon the town. In the room of pallet beds, all but Kirk had at last sunk into sleep. Stiff with the tension of his night-long vigil, he moved among them, waking them. Then he heard the house reverberate to the slam of the front door. It was with no sense of surprise that he also heard Tula's hysterical sobbing. Lindstrom was at the door before him. Kirk put a hand on his shoulder. "Take it easy, Mr. Lindstrom. If she's taking it hard, you'd better take it easy."

They found Tamar with Reger. The father, his face agonized, held the bloody, bedraggled body of his daughter in his arms. She twisted away from him, resisting comfort.

"It's all right now, child. For another year. It's over for another year."

Kirk called, "Bones! You're needed. Get out here!"

As McCoy removed his jet-syringe from his medical kit, Kirk saw the look of anxious inquiry on Reger's face. "It will calm her down," he said quietly. "Trust us, Reger."

Lindstrom, watching, could not contain himself. There was scorching contempt in his voice as he cried, "You didn't even try to bring her home, Reger! What kind of father are you, anyway?"

Reger looked up, his eyes tortured. "It is Landru's will," he said.

"Landru again." Kirk's comment was toneless. "Landru—what about Landru? Who is he?"

Reger and Tamar exchanged terrified glances. Then Tamar said slowly, "It is true, then. You did not attend the festival last night."

"No, we did not," Kirk said.

Reger gave a wild cry. "Then you are not of the Body!" He stared around him as though seeking for some point from which to orient himself in a dissolving world. He made no move as McCoy, noting the effects of his shot, gently moved Tula to a nearby couch where he laid her down. "She's asleep," he said.

Reger approached her, peering at her stilled face. Then he looked at McCoy. "Are you . . . are you . . . Archons?"

"What if we are?" Kirk said.

"It was said more would follow. If you are indeed Archons—"

Tamar cried, "We must hide them! Quickly! The Lawgivers . . ."

"We can take care of ourselves, friend," Kirk told him.

"Landru will know!" Tamar screamed. "He will come!"

The front door crashed open. Two hooded Lawgivers stood on the threshold, Hacom beside them. The old man pointed a shaking finger at Tamar. "He is the one! He mocked the Lawgivers! I heard him!"

Tamar had shrunk back against the wall's support. "No, Hacom . . . it was a joke!"

"The others, too!" cried Hacom. "They were here, but they scorned the festival! I saw it!"

One of the hooded beings spoke. "Tamar . . . stand clear."

Trembling, scarcely able to stand, Tamar bowed his head. "I hear," he said, "and obey the word of Landru."

The Lawgiver lifted his staff, pointing it at Tamar. A tiny dart of flame springing from its end struck straight at his heart. He fell dead.

Stunned, Kirk said, "What—?"

The Lawgiver, ignoring the fallen body between them, addressed Kirk. "You attack the Body. You have heard the word, and disobeyed. You will be absorbed."

He raised his staff again; and Lindstrom, making a swift reach for his phaser, was stopped by a gesture from Kirk.

"What do you mean, absorbed?" he said.

"There! You see?" Hacom's voice was venomous. "They are not of the Body!"

"You will be absorbed," said the Lawgiver. "The good is all. Landru is gentle. You will come."

For the first time the second Lawgiver lifted his staff, pointing it at the *Enterprise* party. Reger spoke, hopelessness dulling his voice. "You must go. It is Landru's will. There is no hope. We must all go with them . . . to the chambers. It happened with the Archons the same way."

Slowly, with deadly deliberation, the two staves swerved to focus on Kirk and Spock. Reger, fatalistically obedient, was moving toward the door when Kirk said, "No. We're not going anywhere."

The stony faces showed no change. The first Lawgiver said, "It is the law. You must come."

Kirk spoke quietly. "I said we're not going anywhere."

The two cowled creatures stared. Then, hesitantly, they moved back a step. After a moment, the first one bent his hood to the other in a whispering conference. Spock, edging to Kirk, said, "Sir, they obviously are not prepared to deal with outright defiance. How did you know?"

"Everything we've seen seems to indicate some sort of compulsion—an involuntary stimulus to action. I just wanted to test it."

"Your analysis seems correct, Captain. But it is a totally abnormal condition."

The two Lawgivers had ended their conference. The first one spoke heavily. "It is plain that you simply did not understand. I will rephrase the order. You are commanded to accompany us to the absorption chambers."

Kirk pointed down at Tamar's crumpled body. "Why did you kill this man?"

"Out of order. You will obey. It is the word of Landru."

"Tell Landru," Kirk said, "that we shall come in our own good time . . . and we will speak to him."

A look of horror filled the stony faces. The first Lawgiver pushed his staff at Kirk. Kirk knocked it from his hand. The creature gaped as it clattered to the floor. Lindstrom picked it up, looked at it briefly, and was handing it to Spock when the Lawgiver, as though listening, whispered, "You . . . cannot. It is Landru."

Both Lawgivers froze. Spock, the staff in hand, spoke to Kirk. "Amazing, Captain. This is merely a hollow tube. No mechanism at all."

Kirk glanced at it. Neither of the Lawgivers gave the slightest sign of having heard. Reger jerked at Kirk's sleeve. "They are communing," he said. "We have a little time. Please come . . . come with me."

"Where to?" Kirk said.

"A place I know of. You'll be safe there." Urgency came into his voice. "But hurry! You must hurry! Landru will come!"

His panic was genuine. After a moment, Kirk signaled his men. They followed Reger out the door, passing the motionless figures of the Lawgivers. Outside, the street was littered with the debris of the festival—shattered glass, rocks, broken clubs, remnants of ripped homespun garments. In the windless air, smoke still hung heavily over a fire-gutted building. But the people who passed were peaceful-looking, their faces again amiable, utterly blank.

"Quite a festival they had," Kirk said. "Mr. Spock, what do you make of all this?"

"It is totally illogical. Last night, without apparent cause or reason, they wrought complete havoc. Yet today . . ."

"*Now*," Kirk said, "they're back to normal." He frowned. "To whatever's normal on this planet. Bilar, for instance. Here he comes as blandly innocent as though he were incapable of roaring like an animal."

Bilar stopped. "Mornin', friends," he said.

Reger returned the greeting and Lindstrom angrily seized his arm. "He's the thing who did that hurt to your daughter! Doesn't that mean anything to you?"

"No," Reger said. "It wasn't Bilar. It was Landru." He shook himself free, turning back to the others. "Hurry! We haven't much time left."

He broke off, staring around him. "It's too late!" he whispered. "Look at them!"

Four passers-by had paused, standing so still they

136

seemed not to breathe. All of them, eyes wide open, were frozen into attitudes of concentrated listening.

"What is it?" Kirk demanded.

"Landru!" Reger said. "He is summoning the Body. See them gathering?"

"Telepathy, Captain," Spock said.

Suddenly people were breaking free of their listening stances to pick up discarded missiles from the littered street. Slowly, like automatons, they began to move toward the *Enterprise* group. In the blankly amiable faces there was something chilling now, mindlessly hostile and deadly.

Kirk said, "Phasers . . . on stun. Which way, Reger?"

Reger hesitated. "Perhaps . . . through there, but Landru . . ."

"We'll handle Landru," Kirk said. "Just get us out of this!"

It was as they moved toward the alley ahead of them that the rocks came hurling against them. A man struck at Spock with a club, the smile on his lips as vacant as his eyes. Then Kirk saw that another armed group had appeared at the far end of the alley. Rocks were flying toward them.

Kirk spoke tersely to Reger. "I don't want to hurt them. Warn them to stay back!"

Reger shook his head despairingly. "They are in the Body! It is Landru!"

Threatening, people were converging on them from both ends of the alley and Kirk, jerking out his phaser, snapped his orders. "Stun only! Wide field! Fire!"

The stun beams spurted from their phasers with a spray effect. The advancing mob fell without a sound. Kirk whirled to confront the rear group. Again, people fell silently. Spock moved to one of the unconscious bodies. "Captain!"

Kirk went over to him. The quiet face that stared blankly up into his was that of Lieutenant O'Neill. He turned to call to his two security crewmen. "Security—over here!" Then he spoke to Reger. "This is one of our men," he said.

"No more," Reger reminded him. "He's been absorbed."

"Nonsense!" Kirk said briskly. "We'll take him along with us, Mr. Spock."

"I tell you he's one of them now!" Reger cried. "When he wakes Landru will find us through him! Leave him here! He's our enemy. He's been absorbed!"

The full implications of the word struck Kirk for the first time. "Absorbed?" he said.

"The Body absorbs its enemies. It kills only when it has to." Reger's voice sank to a terrified whisper. "When the first Archons came, free, out of control, opposing the word of Landru, many were killed. The rest were absorbed. Leave him here. Be wise."

"We take him with us," Kirk said.

Lindstrom spoke. "Captain, now that we've got O'Neill, let's beam out of here."

"Not yet. We still have to find what happened to the Archons. Reger, which way?"

Reger pointed ahead, indicating a left turn at the end of the alley. The Security men picked up O'Neill as the group hurriedly followed Reger's lead. It introduced them into a cellarlike chamber, dark, but bulked with shadowy objects of odds and ends. As the guards set O'Neill down against a wall, Reger crossed to a wall to open a cabinet from which he extracted a flat package, wrapped in rags. Revealed, it turned out to be a translucent panel. A section of it, touched, began to glow with strong light that illuminated the entire room.

Spock said, "Amazing in this culture! I go further. Impossible in this culture!"

Reger turned. "It is from the time before Landru."

"Before Landru? How long ago is that?" Kirk said.

"We do not know positively. Some say . . . as long as six thousand years." Reger spoke with a certain pride. Spock was examining the lighting panel with his tricorder. "I do not identify the metal, Captain. But it took a very advanced technology to construct a device

138

like this. Inconsistent with the rest of the environment."

"But not inconsistent with some of the things we've seen," Kirk said. "Those staffs, those hollow tubes, obviously antennae for some kind of broadcast power. Telepathy—who knows?" He saw the look of astoundedness quiet Spock's face into a more than usual expressionlessness. "What is it, Spock?"

"I am recording immensely strong power generations, Captain . . ."

"Unusual for this area?"

"Incredible for *any* area." Spock leaned closer to his tricorder. "Near here but radiating in all directions—"

A groan from O'Neill broke into his voice. McCoy, looking up from his bent position over the unconscious man, spoke to Kirk. "He's coming around, Jim."

Reger uttered a shout. "He must not! Once he is conscious, Landru will find us. Through him. And if the others come—"

"What others?" Kirk said.

"Those like me . . . and you. Who resist Landru."

"An underground," Spock said. "IIow are you organized?"

"In threes," Reger told him. "Myself . . . Tamar who is dead now . . . and one other."

"Who?" Kirk said.

Reger hesitated. "I don't know. Tamar was the contact."

"Jim," McCoy said, "I need a decision. Another few seconds—"

"He must not regain consciousness!" Reger screamed. "He would destroy us all. He is now of the Body!"

Kirk bit his lip. Then he looked down at O'Neill. "Give him a shot, Bones. Keep him asleep." He whirled on Reger. "I want some answers now. What is the Body?"

"The people. You saw them."

"And the Lawgivers?" Spock asked.

"They are the arms and legs."

"That leaves a brain," Kirk said.

Inflection drained from Reger's voice. "Of course," he said. "Landru." In a mechanical manner as though speaking a lesson learned by rote, he added, "Landru completes the Whole. Unity and Perfection, tranquility and peace."

Spock was eyeing him. "I should say, Captain, that this is a society organized on a physiological concept. One Body, maintained and controlled by the ones known as Lawgivers, directed by one brain . . ."

Kirk said, "A man who—"

"Not necessarily a man, Captain."

Kirk turned to Reger. "This underground of yours. If Landru is so powerful, how do you survive?"

"I do not know. Some of us escape the directives. Not many but some. It was that way with the Archons."

"Tell me about the Archons," Kirk said.

"They refused to accept the will of Landru. But they had invaded the Body. Landru pulled them down from the sky."

Incredulous, Kirk said, "Pull a Starship down?" He turned to Spock. "Those power readings you took before. Are they—"

Spock completed the sentence. "Powerful enough to destroy a Starship? Affirmative, Captain."

They looked at each other for a long moment. Then Kirk flipped out his communicator. "Kirk to *Enterprise.* Come in!"

But it wasn't Uhura who responded. It was Scott, his voice taut with strain. "Captain! We're under attack! Heat beams of some kind. Coming up from the planet's surface!"

"Status report," Kirk said.

"Our shields are holding, but they're taking all our power. If we try to warp out, or even move on impulse engines, we'll lose our shields—and burn up like a cinder!"

"Orbit condition, Scotty?"

"We're going down. Unless those beams get off us

so we can use our engines, we're due to hit atmosphere in less than twelve hours."

Spock came to stand beside him as he said, "Keep your shields up, Scotty. Do everything you can to maintain orbit. We'll try to locate the source of the beams and stop them here. Over."

Static crashed into Scott's reply, drowning his words. ". . . impossible . . . emergency by-pass circuits but . . . whenever you . . . contact . . ."

Kirk turned the gain up, but the static alone grew loud. Spock had unlimbered his tricorder. Now he called, "Captain! Sensor beams! I believe we're being probed." He bent over his device, concentrated. "Yes. Quite strong. And directed here."

"Block them out!" Kirk cried.

"It's Landru!" Reger yelled.

Spock made an adjustment on his tricorder. Then he shook his head. "They're too strong, Captain. I can't block them." He lifted his head suddenly from his tricorder, then whirled to the wall on his left. A low-pitched humming sound was coming from it. Kirk, in his turn, faced the wall. On it a light had begun to glow, coiling and twisting in swirling patterns. They brightened, and at the same moment started to gather into the outline of a figure. It seemed to be collecting substance, the flesh and bone of a handsome elderly man. The eyes had kindness in them and the features, benign, composed, radiated wisdom. It appeared to be regarding them with benevolence. But its face and body kept their strange flowing movement.

The figure on the wall said, "I am Landru."

Reger fell to his knees, groaning in animal terror. Spock, observant, quite unawed, said, "A projection, Captain. Unreal."

"But beautifully executed, Mr. Spock. With no apparatus at this end."

The kindly eyes of the wall man fixed on him. "You have come as destroyers. That is sad. You bring an infection."

141

"You are holding my ship," Kirk said. "I demand you release it."

The mouth went on talking as though the ears had not heard. "You come to a world without hate, without conflict, without fear . . . no war, no disease, no crime, none of the old evils. I, Landru, seek tranquility, peace for all . . . the Universal Good."

This time Kirk shouted. "We come on a mission of peace and goodwill!"

Landru went on, oblivious. "The Good must transcend the Evil. It shall be done. So it has been since the beginning."

"He doesn't hear you, Captain," Spock said.

Lindstrom drew his phaser. "Maybe he'll hear this!"

"No!" Kirk's rebuke was sharp. "That'll do no good." He turned back to the lighted figure. "Landru, listen to us."

"You will be absorbed," said the benign voice. "Your individuality will merge with the Unity of Good. In your submergence into the common being of the Body you will find contentment and fulfillment. You will experience the Absolute Good."

The low-pitched hum had grown louder. Landru smiled tenderly upon them. "There will be a moment of pain, but you will not be harmed. Peace and Good place their blessings upon you."

Kirk took a step toward the image. But the humming abruptly rose to a screeching whine that pierced the ears like a sharpened blade. Reger toppled forward. McCoy and Lindstrom, driven to their knees, held their ears, their eyes shut. One after the other the security crewmen crumpled. Spock and Kirk kept their feet for a moment longer. Then, they, too, the spike of the whine, thrusting deeper into their brains, pitched forward into unconsciousness.

Kirk was the first to recover. He found himself lying on a thin pallet pushed against one of the bare stone walls of a cell. Lifting his head, he saw Lindstrom stir. Getting to his knees, he crawled over to Spock. "Mr. Spock! Mr. Spock!"

Slowly Spock's eyes opened. Kirk bent over Lindstrom, shaking him and the security guard beside him. "Wake up, Lindstrom! Mr. Lindstrom, wake up!"

Spock was on his feet. "Captain! Where's the Doctor?"

"I don't know. He was gone when I came to. So was the other guard."

"From the number of pallets on the floor, sir, I should say they have been here and have been removed."

"Just where is here?" Kirk said.

Spock glanced around. "A maximum-security establishment, obviously. Are you armed, sir?"

"No. All our phasers are gone. I checked." He went to the heavy, bolted door. "Locked," he said.

"My head aches," observed Lindstrom.

"The natural result of being subjected to sub-sonic, Mr. Lindstrom," Spock told him. "Sound waves so controlled as to set up insuperable contradictions in audio impulses. Stronger, they could have killed. As it was, they merely rendered us unconscious."

"That's enough analysis," Kirk said. "Let's start thinking of ways out of here. Mr. Spock, how about that inability of those Lawgivers to cope with the unexpected?"

"I wouldn't count on that happening again, Captain. As well organized as this society seems to be, I cannot conceive of such an oversight going uncorrected." He paused. "Interesting, however. Their reaction to your defiance was remarkably similar to the reactions of a computer—one that's been fed insufficient or contradictory data."

"Are you suggesting that the Lawgivers are mere computers—not human?"

"Quite human, Captain. It's just that all the facts are not yet in. There are gaps—"

He broke off. A rattle had come from the door. Kirk and the others sprang to the alert—and the door opened. A Lawgiver, his staff aimed at them, entered, followed by McCoy and the missing security man.

Both were beaming vacantly, happily. Kirk stared at McCoy, dismay in his face. The Lawgiver left, closing the door behind him. The lock snapped.

"Bones . . ."

McCoy smiled at Kirk. "Hello, friend. They told us to wait here." He started toward a corner pallet, no sign whatever of recognition in his empty eyes.

"Bones!" Kirk cried. "Don't you know me?"

McCoy stared at him in obvious surprise. "We all know one another in Landru, friend."

Spock said, "Just like Sulu, Captain."

Kirk seized McCoy's arm, shaking it. "Think, man!" he cried. "The *Enterprise!* The ship! You remember the ship!"

McCoy shook his head bewilderedly. "You speak very strangely, friend. Are you from far away?"

Kirk's voice was fierce. "Bones, try to remember!"

"Landru remembers," McCoy said. "Ask Landru. He watches. He knows." A flicker of suspicion sharpened his eyes. "You are strange. Are you not of the Body?"

Kirk released his arm with a groan. McCoy at once lost his suspicious look, and, smiling emptily at nothing, moved away to sit down on one of the pallets.

The door opened again to the grinding of freed locks. Two Lawgivers stood in the entrance. One aimed his staff at Kirk. "Come," the cold voice said.

Kirk exchanged a quick glance with Spock. "And what if I don't?" he said.

"Then you will die."

"They have been corrected, Captain," Spock said. "Or reprogrammed. You'd better go with them, sir."

Kirk nodded. "All right. Spock, work on Bones. See if you can—"

"Come!" said the Lawgiver again.

Both staffs were aimed at Kirk as he passed through the cell door. As the heavy door swung to behind him, Spock whirled to McCoy. "Doctor, what will they do to him?"

McCoy smirked at him beatifically. "He goes to Joy.

144

He goes to Peace and Tranquility. He goes to meet Landru. Happiness is to all of us who are blessed by Landru."

The room to which the Lawgivers were escorting Kirk was of stone—a room he was to remember as the "absorption chamber". A niche in a wall was equipped with a control panel. As he was prodded into the room, Kirk saw that another Lawgiver stood at the niche. Against another wall a manacle hung from a chain. Kirk was shoved toward it, one of his captors holding him while the other fastened the gyve about his wrist. Then they turned and left the room. Their footsteps had barely ceased to echo on the stone floor of the corridor outside when a fourth Lawgiver entered. He didn't so much as glance at Kirk but moved to his fellow at the control panel, nodding curtly.

Finally, he turned. "I am Marplon," he said. "It is your hour. Happy communing."

The Lawgiver at the panel bowed. "With thanks," he said. "Happy communing." Then, like the others, he left the absorption room. Alone now, Marplon faced Kirk. It seemed to Kirk that his visage resembled a death mask. But Marplon could move. When he had he placed a headset over his hood, his hands touched the control panel with the authority derived from much experience. The room flooded with bright, flashing colors; a humming sound began. The lights were blinding and the sound seemed to echo itself in Kirk's head. He twisted in his bonds.

At the same moment, back in the detention cell, Lindstrom was pacing it angrily. He halted to confront Spock. "Are we just going to stay here?"

"There seems to be little else we can do," Spock told him mildly. "Unless you can think of a way to get through that locked door."

"This is ridiculous! Prisoners of a bunch of Stone Age characters running around in robes."

"And apparently commanding powers far beyond our comprehension. Not simple, Mr. Lindstrom. Not ridiculous. Very, very dangerous."

On his last word the cell door opened and the two Lawgivers who had apprehended Kirk walked in. This time they aimed their staffs at Spock.

"You," said the spokesman. "Come."

For a fleeting second, Spock hesitated. The tip of one of the staffs quivered. Spock took his place between his guards. They led him out. They led him out and down the corridor to the absorption chamber. Kirk greeted him, an imbecile smile on his face.

"Captain!"

"Joy be with you, friend. Peace and contentment will fill you. You will know the peace of Landru . . ."

Then unguarded, alone, Kirk moved quietly to the door of the room with the manacle. The Lawgivers gave way as he passed. Spock stared after him, a horror only to be read by the absolute impassivity in his face.

He wasn't left much time to indulge it. Already they were manacling him to the wall. But the Vulcan's inveterate curiosity, not to be subdued, was already subordinating this personal experience to interest in the control panel's mechanism. As with Kirk, the two shackling Lawgivers, as soon as their task was accomplished, left. Marplon threw a switch on his panel. The colored lights began to swirl. Spock watched their coiling flashes with interest.

"Show no surprise," Marplon said. "The effect is harmless."

Spock looked at Marplon. The Lawgiver spoke in a lowered voice. "My name is Marplon. I was too late to save your first two friends. They have been absorbed. Beware of them."

"And my Captain?"

"He is unharmed," said Marplon. "Unchanged." He moved a finger; the light glowed brighter, and the hum grew more shrill. Marplon left his console to release Spock from his manacle. "I am the third man in Reger's trio," he said. "We have been waiting for your return."

"We are not Archons, Marplon," Spock said.

"Whatever you call yourselves, you are in fulfillment of prophecy. We ask for your help."

Spock said, "Where is Reger?"

"He will join us. He is immune to the absorption. Hurry! Time is short."

"Who is Landru?"

Marplon recoiled. "I cannot answer your questions now."

"Why not?" Spock said.

"Landru! He will hear!" Marplon went swiftly to his console, and reaching down and inward, brought out the ship's company's phasers. Spock, seizing several of them, stowed them away. As the last phaser was secreted, two Lawgivers pushed the door open.

"It is done," Marplon told them.

Spock assumed the idiotically amiable look of the anointed. "Joy be with you," he said.

"Landru is all," said the Lawgivers in unison. Spock moved past them and into the corridor. Making his way back to the cell, he found Kirk there, smiling blankly into space. Two Lawgivers pushed past him to beckon to the security crewman who had not been treated. Ashen with fear, he rose and went with them.

Spock went to Kirk. "Captain . . ."

"Peace and tranquility to you, friend," Kirk said. Then, in a lowered voice, he added, "Spock, you all right?"

"Quite all right, sir. Be careful of Dr. McCoy."

"I understand. Landru?"

"I am formulating an opinion, Captain."

"And?"

"Not here. The Doctor . . ."

But McCoy was already rising from his pallet, staring at them. His amiable smile faded and the look of curiosity on his face gave it a peculiar threatening aspect. "You speak in whispers," he said. "This is not the way of Landru."

"Joy to you, friend," Kirk said. "Tranquility be yours."

"And peace and harmony," intoned McCoy. "Are you of the Body?"

"The Body is one," Kirk said.

"Blessed be the Body. Health to all its parts." Mc-

147

Coy was smiling again, apparently satisfied. He sank back on the pallet; Kirk and Spock, joining him on theirs, sat on them in such a way as to screen their faces from McCoy. Then, in the same carefully lowered voice, he said, "What's your theory, Mr. Spock?"

"This is a soulless society, Captain. It has no spirit, no spark. All is indeed peace and tranquility, the peace of the factory, the machine's tranquility . . . all parts working in unison."

"I've noticed that the routine is disturbed if something unexplained happens."

"Until new orders are received. The question is, who gives those orders?"

"Landru," Kirk said.

"There is no Landru," Spock said. "Not in the human sense."

"You're thinking the same way I am, Mr. Spock."

"Yes, Captain. But as to what we must do . . ."

"We must pull out the plug, Mr. Spock."

"Sir?"

"Landru must die."

Spock's left eyebrow lifted. "Our prime directive of non-interference," he began.

"That refers to a living, growing culture. I'm not convinced that this one can qualify as—" He broke off as the cell door opened. Marplon and Reger, carrying the confiscated communicators, entered. "It is the gift of Landru to you," Marplon said. The words were addressed to McCoy and the treated security guard. They smiled vacantly and McCoy said, "Joy to you, friends." He leaned back against the stone wall, his eyes closed. Reger and Marplon hurried past him to Kirk and Spock.

"We brought your signaling devices," Marplon told Kirk. "You may need them."

"What we really need is more information about Landru," Kirk said.

Reger shrank back. "Prophecy says—" Marplon began.

148

"Never mind what prophecy says! If you want to be liberated from Landru, you have to help us!"

Spock cut in warningly. "Captain . . ."

McCoy was moving toward them, open and hostile suspicion in his face. "I heard you!" he cried. "You are not of the Body!" He hurled himself on Kirk, reaching for his throat. Spock tried to pry him off only to be taken in the rear by the treated security guard. "Lawgivers!" McCoy shouted. "Here are traitors! Traitors!"

With a twist, Kirk freed himself, crying, "Bones! Bones, I don't want to hurt you! Sit down and be still!"

But McCoy was still screaming, "Lawgivers! Hurry!"

Kirk's blow caught him squarely on the chin. As he fell, the door was flung wide and two Lawgivers, staffs ready, rushed in. At once they were jumped by Kirk and Spock. Kirk dropped his man with a hard wallop at the back of the neck while Spock applied the Vulcan neck pinch to his. Reger and Marplon, pressed against the wall, were staring at the fallen Lawgivers in horror.

Hurriedly, Kirk started disrobing the man he had downed. As Spock did the same to his, Kirk, donning the cowled garment, snapped at the others. "Where is Landru?"

"No," Marplon said. "No, no . . ."

"Where do we find him?" Kirk demanded.

"He will find us!" cried Reger. "He will destroy!"

Kirk whirled on Marplon. "You said you wanted a chance to help. All right, you're getting it! Where is he? You're a Lawgiver! Where do you see him?"

"We never see him. We hear him. In the Hall of Audiences!"

"In this building?"

Marplon nodded, terrified. Kirk let his rage rip. "You're going to take us there! Snap out of it, both of you! Start behaving like men!"

Spock opened a communicator. "Spock to *Enterprise*. Status report!"

"Mr. Spock!" It was Scott's voice. "I've been trying to reach you!"

"Report, Mr. Scott!"

"Orbit still decaying, sir. Give it six hours, more or less. Heat rays still on us. You've got to cut them off—or we'll cook one way or another."

Nodding at Spock, Kirk took the communicator. "Stand by, Mr. Scott. We're doing what we can. How's Mr. Sulu?"

"Peaceful enough, but he worries me."

"Put a guard on him."

"On Sulu?" Scott was shocked.

"That's an order! Watch him! Captain out!"

Robed now and armed, Kirk and Spock turned to Marplon and Reger. "All right. Now about Landru . . ."

"He made us!" Marplon cried. "He made this world!"

Reger was on his knees. "Please. We have gone too far! Don't—"

Spock said, "You say Landru made this world. Explain."

"There was war . . . six thousand years ago there was war . . . and convulsion. The world was destroying itself. Landru was our leader. He saw the truth. He changed the world. He took us back, back to a simple time, of peace, of tranquility."

"What happened to him?" Kirk said.

"He still lives!" cried Marplon. "He is here now! He sees . . . he hears . . . we have destroyed ourselves . . . please, please, no more."

Kirk spoke very softly. "You said you wanted freedom. It is time you learned that freedom is not a gift. You have to earn it—or you don't get it. Come on! We're going to find Landru!"

Reger stumbled to his knees. "No . . . no. I was wrong!" Wringing his hands, his eyes upturned imploringly, he shrieked, "I submit . . . I bare myself to the will of Landru."

Kirk seized his shoulder. "It is too late for that! But Reger, shaking himself loose, dashed to the door, screaming, "No! No! Lawgivers! Help me!" Spock, reaching out, gave him the neck pinch. He fell; Marplon, staring, slowly turned to meet Kirk's eyes.

"All right, my friend," Kirk said. "It's up to you now. Take us to Landru."

"He will strike us down," said Marplon.

"Maybe—or it might be the other way around. Mr. Lindstrom, stay here and take care of Dr. McCoy. Let's go, Mr. Spock." He grabbed Marplon's arm, propelling him to the door. Dismay and fear on his face, Marplon opened it, and Kirk's hand still on his arm, he moved out into the corridor. From under his hood, Kirk could see two robed Lawgivers approaching. They passed without so much as glancing at the three figures they assumed to be fellow Lawgivers. The trio moved on down the corridor and Kirk saw that it ended at a large imposing door.

Marplon paused in front of it, visibly trembling. "This is . . . the Hall of Audiences," he whispered.

"Do you have a key?"

At Marplon's nod, Kirk said, "Open it."

"But—it is Landru . . ."

"Open it," Kirk said again. But he had to take the key from Marplon's trembling hands to open it himself. The Hall of Audiences was a large room, completely bare. In one of the walls was set a glowing panel. Marplon pointed to it. "Landru—he speaks here . . ." he whispered.

Kirk stepped forward. "Landru! We are the Archons!" he said. The moldy, cold silence in the big room remained unbroken. Kirk spoke again. "We are the Archons. We've come to talk with you!"

Very gradually the wise, impressive, benevolent face they remembered began to take shape on the panel. In an extremity of panic, Marplon broke into sobs, prostrating himself. "Landru comes!" he wept. "He comes!"

The noble figure was completed now, a warm half smile on its lips. They opened. "Despite my efforts not to harm you, you have invaded the Body. You are causing great harm."

"We have no intention of causing harm," Kirk said.

Landru continued as though Kirk had not spoken.

151

"Obliteration is necessary. The infection is strong. For the good of the Body, you must die. It is a great sorrow."

"We do not intend to die!"

The oblivious voice continued, kind, gently. "All who have seen you, who know of your presence, must be excised. The memory of the Body must be cleansed."

"Listen to me!" Kirk shouted.

"Captain . . . useless," Spock said. "A projection!"

"All right, Mr. Spock! Let's have a look at the projector!"

They whipped out their phasers simultaneously, turning their beams on the glowing panel. There was a great flash of blinding light. The figure of Landru vanished and the light in the panel faded. But the real Landru had not disappeared. Behind the panel he survived in row upon row of giant computers—a vast complex of dials, switches, involved circuits all quietly operating.

"It had to be," Kirk said. "Landru."

"Of course, Captain. A machine. This entire society is a machine's idea of perfection. Peace, harmony . . ."

"And no soul."

Suddenly the machine buzzed. A voice spoke. It said, "I am Landru. You have intruded."

"Pull out its plug, Mr. Spock."

They aimed their phasers. But before they could fire, there came another buzzing from the machine and a flash of light immobilized their weapons. "Your devices have been neutralized," said the voice. "So it shall be with you. I am Landru."

"Landru died six thousand years ago," Kirk said.

"I am Landru!" cried the machine. "I am he. All that he was, I am. His experience, his knowledge—"

"But not his wisdom," Kirk said. "He may have programmed you, but he could not give you his soul."

"Your statement is irrelevant," said the voice. "You will be obliterated. The good of the Body is the primal essence."

152

"That's the answer, Captain," Spock said. "That good of the Body . . ."

Kirk nodded. "What is the good?" he asked.

"I am Landru."

"Landru is dead. You are a machine. A question has been put to you. Answer it!"

Circuits hummed. "The good is the harmonious continuation of the Body," said the voice. "The good is peace, tranquility, harmony. The good of the Body is the prime directive."

"I put it to you that you have disobeyed the prime directive—that you are harmful to the Body."

The circuits hummed louder. "The Body is . . . it exists. It is healthy."

"It is dying," Kirk said. "You are destroying it."

"Do you ask a question?" queried the voice.

"What have you done to do justice to the full potential of every individual of the Body?"

"Insufficient data. I am not programmed to answer that question."

"Then program yourself," Spock said. "Or are your circuits limited?"

"My circuits arc unlimited. I will reprogram."

The machine buzzed roughly. A screech came from it. Marplon, on the floor, was getting to his feet, his eyes staring at the massive computer face. As he gained them, two more Lawgivers appeared, staffless.

They approached the machine. "Landru!" cried one. "Guide us! Landru?" His voice was a wail.

Kirk had whirled to cover them with his phaser when Spock raised his hand. "Not necessary, Captain. They have no guidance . . . possibly for the first time in their lives."

Kirk, lowering his phaser, turned back to the machine. "Landru! Answer that question!"

The voice had a metallic tone now. "Peace, order, and tranquility are maintained. The Body lives. But creativity is mine. Creativity is necessary for the health of the Body." It buzzed again. "This is impossible. It is a paradox. It shall be resolved."

Marplon spoke at last. "Is that truly Landru?"

"What's left of him," Spock said. "What's left of him after he built this machine and programmed it six thousand years ago."

Kirk addressed the machine. "Landru! The paradox!"

The humming fell dead. The voice, dully metallic now, said, "It will not resolve."

"You must create the good," Kirk said. "That is the will of Landru—nothing else . . ."

"But there is evil," said the voice.

"Then the evil must be destroyed. It is the prime directive. You are the evil."

The machine resumed its humming—a humming broken by hard, harsh clicks. Lights flashed wildly. "I think! I live!" said the machine.

"You say you are Landru!" Kirk shouted. "Then create the good! Destroy evil! Fulfill the prime directive!"

The hum rose to a roar. A drift of smoke wafted up from a switch. Then a shower of sparks burst from the machine's metal face—and with the blast of exploding circuits, all its lights went out.

Kirk turned to the three awed Lawgivers. "All right, you can get rid of those robes now. If I were you, I'd start looking for real jobs." He opened the communicator. "Kirk to *Enterprise*. Come in, please."

Scott's voice was loud with relief. "Captain, are you all right?"

"Never mind about us. What about you?"

"The heat rays have gone, and Mr. Sulu's back to normal."

"Excellent, Mr. Scott. Stand by to beam-up landing party." He returned the communicator to Spock. "Let's see what the others are doing, Mr. Spock. Mr. Marplon can finish up here."

His command chair seemed to welcome Kirk. He'd never thought of it as comfortable before. But he stretched in it, hands locked behind his neck as Spock left his station to stand beside him while he dictated his last notation into his Captain's log. "Sociologist Lindstrom is remaining behind on Beta 3000 with a party of experts who will help restore the culture to a human form. Kirk out."

Spock spoke thoughtfully. "Still, Captain, the late Landru was a marvelous feat of engineering. Imagine a computer capable of directing—literally directing—every act of millions of human beings."

"But only a machine, Mr. Spock. The original Landru programmed it with all his knowledge but he couldn't give it his wisdom, his compassion, his understanding—his soul, Mr. Spock."

"Sometimes you are predictably metaphysical, Captain. I prefer the concrete, the graspable, the provable."

"You would make a splendid computer, Mr. Spock."

Spock bowed. "That's very kind of you, sir."

Uhura spoke from behind them. "Captain . . . Mr. Lindstrom from the surface."

Kirk pushed a button. "Yes, Mr. Lindstrom."

"Just wanted to say good-bye, Captain."

"How are things going?"

"Couldn't be better!" The youngster's enthusiasm was like a triumphant shout in his ear. "Already this morning we've had half-a-dozen domestic quarrels and two genuine knock-down drag-outs. It may not be paradise—but it's certainly . . ."

"Human?" asked Kirk.

"Yes! And they're starting to think for themselves! Just give me and our people a few months and we'll have a going society on our hands!"

"One question, Mr. Lindstrom: Landru wanted to give his people peace and security and so programmed the machine. Then how do we account for so total an anomaly as the festival?"

"Sir, with the machine destroyed, we'll never have enough data to answer that one with any confidence—but I have a guess, and I feel almost certain it's the right one. Landru wanted to eliminate war, crime, disease, even personal dissension, and he succeeded. But he failed to allow for population control, and

155

without that even an otherwise static society would soon suffer a declining standard of living, and eventual outright hunger. Clearly Landru wouldn't have wanted that either, but he made no allowances for it.

"So the machine devised its own: one night a year in which all forms of control were shut off, every moral law abrogated; even ordinary human decency was canceled out. One night of the worst kind of civil war, in which *every* person is the enemy of *every* other. I have no proof of this at all, sir—but it's just the sort of solution you'd expect from a machine, and furthermore, a machine that had been programmed to think of people as cells in a Body, of no importance at all as individuals." Suddenly Lindstrom's voice shook. "One night a year of total cancer . . . horrible! I hope I'm dead wrong, but there are precedents."

"That can hardly be fairly characterized as a guess," Spock said. "Ordinarily I do not expect close reasoning from sociologists, but from what I know of the way computers behave when they are given directives supported by insufficient data, I can find no flaw in Mr. Lindstrom's analysis. It should not distress him, for if it is valid—as I am convinced it is—he is indeed just the man to put it right."

"Thank you, Mr. Spock," Lindstrom's voice said. "I'll cherish that. Captain, do you concur?"

"I do indeed," Kirk said. "I have human misgivings which I know you share with me. All I can say now is it sounds promising. Good luck. Kirk out."

Kirk turned to his First Officer and looked at him in silence for a long time. At last he said, "Mr. Spock, if I didn't know you were above such human weaknesses as feelings of solemnity, I'd say you looked solemn. Are you feeling solemn, Mr. Spock?"

"I was merely meditating, sir. I was reflecting on the frequency with which mankind has wished for a world as peaceful and secure as the one Landru provided."

"Quite so, Mr. Spock. And see what happens when we get it! It's our luck and our curse that we're forced to grow, whether we like it or not."

"I have heard human beings say also, Captain, that it is also our joy."

"*Our* joy, Mr. Spock?"

There was no response, but, Kirk thought, Spock knew as well as any man that ancient human motto: *Silence gives assent.*

THE IMMUNITY SYNDROME

(Robert Sabaroff)

White beaches . . . suntanned women . . . mountains, their trout streams just asking for it . . . the lift of a surfboard to a breaking wave . . . familiar tree-shapes —that was shore leave on Starbase Six. And the exhausted crew of the *Enterprise* was on its way to it, unbelievably nearing it at long last. Kirk, remembering the taste of an open-air breakfast of rainbow trout, turned to give Sulu his final approach orders.

"Message from the base, sir," Uhura called. "Heavy interference. All I could get was the word '*Intrepid*' and what sounded like a sector coordinate."

"Try them on another channel, Lieutenant."

McCoy said, "The *Intrepid* is manned by Vulcans only, isn't it, Jim?"

"I believe so." Kirk swung his chair around. "The crew of the *Intrepid* is Vulcan, isn't it, Mr. Spock? I seem to remember the Starship was made entirely Vulcan as a tribute to the skill of your people in arranging that truce with the Romulan Federation. It was an unusual honor."

Spock didn't answer. He didn't turn. But he'd straightened in his chair. Something in the movement disturbed Kirk. He got up and went over to the library-computer station. "Mr. Spock!" Still Spock sat, unmoving, silent. Kirk shook his shoulder. "Spock, what's wrong? Are you in pain?"

"The *Intrepid* is dead. I just felt it die."

Kirk looked at McCoy. McCoy shook his head, shrugging.

"Mr. Spock, you're tired," Kirk said. "Let Chekov take over your station."

"And the four hundred Vulcans aboard her are dead," Spock said.

McCoy said, "Come down to Sickbay, Spock."

Stone-faced, Spock said, "I am quite all right, Doctor. I know what I feel."

Kirk said, "Report to Sickbay, Mr. Spock. That's an order."

"Yes, Captain."

Kirk watched them move to the elevator. They'd all had it. Too many missions. Even Spock's superb stamina had its breaking point. Too many rough missions—and Vulcan logic itself could turn morbidly visionary. It was high time for shore leave.

"Captain, I have Starbase Six now," Uhura said.

Back in his chair, Kirk flipped a switch. "Kirk here. Go ahead."

The bridge speaker spoke. "The last reported position of the Starship *Intrepid* was sector three nine J. You will divert immediately."

Kirk rubbed a hand over his chin before he reached for his own speaker. "The *Enterprise* has just completed the last of several very strenuous missions. The crew is tired. We're on our way for R and R. There must be another Starship in that sector."

"Negative. This is a rescue priority order. We have lost all contact with solar system Gamma Seven A. The *Intrepid* was investigating. Contact has now been lost with the *Intrepid*. Report progress."

"Order acknowledged," Kirk said. "Kirk out."

Sulu was staring at him in questioning dismay. Kirk snapped, "You heard the order, Mr. Sulu. Lay in a course for Gamma Seven A."

Chekov spoke from his console. Awe subdued his voice.

"Solar System Gamma Seven A is dead, Captain. My long-range scan of it shows—"

"Dead? What are you saying, Mr. Chekov? That is a fourth-magnitude star! Its system supports billions of inhabitants! Check your readings!"

"I have, sir. Gamma Seven A is dead."

In Sickbay Spock was saying, "I assure you, Doctor, I am quite all right. The pain was momentary."

McCoy sighed as he took his last diagnostic reading. "My instruments appear to agree with you if I can trust them with a crazy Vulcan anatomy. By the way, how can you be so sure the *Intrepid* is destroyed?"

"I felt it die," his patient said tonelessly.

"But I thought you had to be in physical contact with a subject to sense—"

"Dr. McCoy, even I, a half Vulcan, can sense the death screams of four hundred Vulcan minds crying out over distance between us."

McCoy shook his head. "It's beyond me."

Spock was shouldering back into his shirt. "I have noticed this insensitivity among wholly human beings. It is easier for you to feel the death of one fellow-creature than to feel the deaths of millions."

"Suffer the deaths of thy neighbors, eh, Spock? Is that what you want to wish on us?"

"It might have rendered your history a bit less bloody."

The intercom beeped. "Kirk here. Bones, is Spock all right? If he is, I need him on the bridge."

"Coming, Captain." Kirk met him at the elevator. "You may have been right. Contact with the *Intrepid* has been lost. It has also been lost with an entire solar system. Our scans show that Gamma Seven A is a dead star system."

"That is considerable news." Spock hurried over to his station and Kirk spoke to Uhura. "Any update from Starfleet?"

"I can't filter out the distortions. They're getting worse, sir."

A red light flashed on Sulu's panel. "Captain, the deflector shields just snapped on!"

"Slow down to warp three!" Kirk walked back to Spock. The Vulcan straightened from his stoop over his computer. "Indications of energy turbulence ahead, sir. Unable to analyze. I have never encountered such readings before."

The drama latent in the statement was so uncharacteristic of Spock that Kirk whirled to the main viewing screen. "Magnification factor three on screen!" he ordered.

Star-filled space—the usual vista. "Scan sector," he said. The starfield merely revealed itself from another angle and Sulu said, "Just what are we looking for, Captain?"

"I would assume," Spock said, *"that."*

A black shadow, roughly circular, had appeared on the screen.

"An interstellar dust cloud," Chekov suggested.

Kirk shook his head. "The stars have disappeared. They could be seen through a dust cloud, Mr. Chekov. How do you read it, Mr. Spock?"

"Analysis still eludes me, Captain. Sensors are feeding data to computers now. But whatever that dark zone is, my calculations place it directly on the course that would have brought it into contact with the *Intrepid* and the Gamma Seven A system."

"Are you saying it caused their deaths, Mr. Spock?"

"A possibility, Captain."

After a moment, Kirk nodded. "Hold present course but slow to warp factor one," he told Sulu. "Mr. Chekov, prepare to launch telemetry probe into that zone."

"Aye, sir." Chekov moved controls on his console. "Probe ready. Switching data feed to library-computer."

"Launch probe," Kirk said.

Chekov shoved a stud. "Probe launched."

An ear-shattering blast of static burst from the communications station. Its noise swelled into a crackling roar so fierce that it seemed to possess a physical substance—the substance and force of a giant's slap. It ended as abruptly as it had come. Uhura, dizzy, disoriented, was clinging to her chair.

"And what channel did *that* come in on?" Kirk said.

She had to make a visible effort to answer. "Telemetry . . . the channel from the probe, sir. There's no signal . . . at all now . . ."

"Mr. Spock, speculations?"

"I have none, Captain." Then Spock had leaped from his chair. Uhura, her arms dropped, limp, was slumped over her console. "Lieutenant!" He reached an arm around her, steadying her. "Dizzy," she whispered. "I'll . . . be all right in a minute."

The intercom beeped to McCoy's voice. "Jim, half the women on this ship have fainted. Reports in from all decks."

Kirk glanced at Uhura. "Maybe you'd better check Lieutenant Uhura. She just pulled out of a faint."

"Unless she's out now, keep her up there. I've got an emergency here."

"What's wrong?"

"Nothing organic. Just weakness, nervousness."

"Can you handle it?"

'I can give them stimulants to keep them on their feet."

A tired crew—and now this. Kirk looked at the screen. It offered no cheer. The black shadow now owned almost all of the screen. Hold position here, Mr. Sulu." He got up from his chair—and was hit by an attack of vertigo. He fought it down. "Mr. Spock, I want an update on that shadow ahead of us."

"No analysis, sir. Insufficient information."

Kirk smacked the computer console. "Mr. Spock. I have asked you three times for data on that thing and you have been unable to supply it. 'Insufficient information' won't do. It is your responsibility to deliver sufficient information at all times."

"I am aware of that, sir. But there is nothing in the computer banks on this phenomenon. It is beyond all previous experience."

Kirk looked at the hand that had struck Spock's console. "Weakness, nervousness." He was guilty on both counts. Even Spock couldn't elicit data from the computer banks that hadn't been put into them. "Sorry, Mr. Spock. Something seems to be infecting

162

the entire ship. Let's go for reverse logic. If you can't tell me what that zone of darkness is, tell me what it isn't."

"It is not gaseous, liquid nor solid, despite the fact we can't see through it. It is not a galactic nebula like the Coal Sack. As it has activated our deflector shields, it seems to consist of some energy form—but none that the sensors can identify."

"And you said it is possible it killed the *Intrepid* and that solar system?"

"Yes, Captain."

Kirk turned to Uhura. "Lieutenant, inform Starfleet of our position and situation. Relay all relative information from computer banks." He paused. "Tell them we intend to probe further into the zone of darkness to gain further information."

"Yes, sir."

As he started back to his chair, he swayed under another wash of dizziness. Spock moved to him quickly and he clung for a moment to the muscular arm. "Thank you, Mr. Spock," he said. "I can make it now." He reached his chair. "Distance to the zone of darkness, Mr. Sulu?"

"One hundred thousand kilometers."

"Slow ahead, Mr. Sulu. Impulse power."

His head was still whirling. "Distance now, Mr. Sulu?"

"We penetrate the zone in one minute seven seconds, sir."

"Mr. Chekov, red alert. Stand by, phasers. Full power to deflector shields."

"Phasers standing by—deflectors at full power, sir."

Sound was emitted. It came slowly at first—and not from the communications station. It came from everywhere; and as it built, its mounting tides of invisible shock waves reached everywhere. Their reverberations struck through the metal walls of the engineering section, rushing Scott to check his equipment. Horrified by his readings, he ran to his power levers to test them. Then, mercifully, the all-pervading racket subsided. Up on the bridge, his hands still pressed to his ears, Sulu cried, "Captain—the screen!"

Blackness, total, had claimed it.

"Malfunction, Mr. Spock?"

"No, Captain. All systems working."

Kirk shook his head, trying to clear it. Around him people were still clutching at console rails for support. Kirk struck the intercom button. "Bones, things any better in Sickbay?"

"Worse. They're backed up into the corridor."

"Got anything that will help up here? I don't want anyone on the bridge folding at a critical moment."

"On my way. McCoy out."

Kirk pushed the intercom button again. "Kirk to Engineering. The power's dropped, Mr. Scott! What's happened?"

"We've lost five points of our energy reserve. The deflector shields have been weakened."

"Can you compensate, Scotty?"

"Yes, if we don't lose any more. Don't ask me how it happened."

Kirk spoke sharply. "I *am* asking you, mister. I need answers!"

McCoy's answer was an air-hypo. He hurried into the bridge with a nurse. As Kirk accepted the hissing injection, McCoy said, "It's a stimulant, Jim." As he adjusted the hypo for Sulu's shot, Kirk said, "Just how bad is it, Bones?"

"Two thirds of personnel are affected."

"This is a sick ship, Bones. We're picking up problems faster than we can solve them. It's as though we were in the middle of some creeping paralysis."

"Maybe we are," McCoy said. He left the command chair to continue his round with the hypo. Kirk got up to go to the computer station. "Mr. Spock, any analysis of that last noise outburst—the one that started to lose us power?"

Spock nodded. "The sound was the turbulence caused by our penetration of a boundary layer."

"What sort of boundary layer?"

"I don't know, Captain."

"Boundary between what and what?"

"Between where we were and where we are." At Kirk's stare, he went on. "I still have no specifics, sir. But we seem to have entered an area of energy that is not compatible with life or mechanical processes. As we move on, the source of it will grow stronger— and we will grow weaker."

"Recommendations?"

McCoy spoke. "I recommend survival, Jim. Let's get out of here." He turned and walked to the elevator, the nurse behind him.

Kirk faced around to the questioning faces. And Starbase had demanded a "progress" report. Progress to what? The fate of the *Intrepid*—the billions of lives that had once breathed on Gamma Seven A? Bureaucracy . . . evasion by comfortable chairs.

He walked slowly back to his uncomfortable chair. The intercom button—yes. "This is the Captain speaking," he said. "We have entered an area that is unfamiliar to us. All hands were tired to begin with and we've all sustained something of a shock. But we've had stimulants. Our deflectors are holding. We've got a good ship. And we know what our mission is. Let's get on with the job. Kirk out."

His own intercom button beeped. "Sickbay to Captain."

"Kirk. Go ahead, Bones."

Before he went ahead, McCoy glanced at the semiconscious Yeoman lying on his diagnostic couch. "Jim, one after another . . . life energy levels . . . my indicators . . ."

Kirk spoke quietly. "Say it, Bones."

"We are dying," McCoy said. "My life monitors show that we are all, each one of us, dying."

The sweat of his own weakness broke from Kirk's pores. He could feel it run cold down his chest.

But the ordeal of the *Enterprise* had just begun. Kirk, down in Engineering, was flung against a mounded dynamo at a sudden lurch of the ship. "And that? What was that, Mr. Scott?"

"An accident, sir. We went into reverse."

"Reverse? That was a *forward* lurch! How could that occur in reverse thrust?"

"I don't know, sir. All I know is that our power levels are draining steadily. They're down to twelve percent. I've never experienced anything like it before."

Spock came in on the intercom. "Captain, we are accelerating. The zone of darkness is pulling us toward it."

"Pulling us? How, Mr. Spock?"

"I don't know. However, I suggest that Mr. Scott give us reverse power."

"Mr. Spock, he just *gave* us reverse power!"

"Then I reverse my suggestion, sir. Ask him to apply a forward thrust."

"Mr. Scott, you heard that. Let's try the forward thrust."

The Engineering Chief shook his head. "I don't know, sir. It contradicts all the rules of logic."

"Logic is Mr. Spock's specialty."

"Yes, sir, but—"

"Nudge it slowly into forward thrust, Mr. Scott."

Scott carefully advanced three controls. Eyeing his instruments anxiously, he relaxed. "That did it, Captain. We're slowing now. But the forward movement hasn't stopped. We're still being pulled ahead."

"Keep applying the forward thrust against the pull. Have one of your men monitor these instruments."

Instruments in Sickbay were being monitored, too. Nurse Chapel, watching her life function indicators, called, "Doctor, they're showing another sharp fall." McCoy, whirling to look, muttered, "Stimulants. How long can we keep them up?" He was checking the panel when Kirk's voice came from the intercom. "This is the Captain speaking. All department heads will report to the Briefing Room in ten minutes. They will come with whatever information gathered on this zone of darkness we are in."

McCoy took his gloom with him to the Briefing Room. Slamming some tape cartridges down on the table, he said, "My sole contribution is the fact that the further we move into this zone of darkness, the weaker our life functions get. I have no idea why." Reaching for a chair, he staggered slightly.

"Bones . . ."

He waved the solicitude aside. "I'm all right. All those stimulants—they catch up with you."

Scott spoke. "As far as the power levels are concerned, everything's acting backwards. But the drain is continuing. And we're still being dragged forward."

"Mr. Spock?" Kirk said.

"I am assuming that something within the zone absorbs both biological and mechanical energy. It would appear to be the same thing that sucked energy from an entire solar system—and the Starship *Intrepid*."

"Some *thing*, Mr. Spock? Not the zone itself?"

"I would say not, Captain. Analysis of the zone suggests it is a negative energy field, however illogical that may sound. *But it is not the source of the power drains.*"

"A shield, then," Kirk said. "An outer layer of protection for something else."

"But what?" Scott said.

"It's pulling the life out of us, whatever it is," McCoy grunted.

"We'll find out what it is," Kirk said. "But first we have to get out of here ourselves." He leaned across the table. "Mr. Scott, forward thrust slowed down our advance before. If you channel all warp and impulse power into one massive forward thrust, it might snap us out of the zone."

Scott's face lightened. "Aye, Captain. I'll reserve enough for the shields in case we don't get out."

Spock's voice was as expressionless as his face. "I submit, Mr. Scott, that if we do not get out, the shields would merely prolong our wait for death."

Kirk regarded him somberly. "Yes. You will apply all power as needed to get us out of here, Mr. Scott. Report to your stations, everybody, and continue your research. Dismissed."

As they left, he remained seated, head bowed on

his hand. At the door Spock stopped, and came back to stand, waiting, at the table. Kirk looked up at him. "The *Intrepid*'s crew would have done all these things, Captain," Spock said. "They were destroyed."

Kirk drummed his fingers on the table. "They may not have done all these things. You've just told us what an illogical situation this is."

"True, sir. It is also true that they never discovered what killed them."

"How can you know that?"

"Vulcan has not been conquered within its collective memory. It is a memory that goes so far back no Vulcan can any longer conceive of a conqueror. I know the ship was defeated because I sensed its death."

"What was it exactly you felt, Mr. Spock?"

"Astonishment. Profound astonishment."

"My Vulcan friend," Kirk said. He got up. "Let's get back to the bridge."

Engineering was calling him as they came out of the elevator. Hurrying to his chair, Kirk pushed the intercom stud. "Kirk here, Scotty."

"We've completed arrangements, sir. I'm ready to try it when you are."

"We've got the power to pull it off?"

The voice was glum. "I hope so, Captain."

"Stand by, Scotty." He pushed another button. "All hands, this is the Captain speaking. An unknown force is pulling us deeper into the zone of darkness. We will apply all available power in one giant forward thrust in the hope it will yank us out of the zone. Prepare yourselves for a big jolt." He buzzed Engineering. "Ready, Mr. Scott. Let's get on with it. *Now!*"

They were prepared for the jolt. And it was big. But what they weren't prepared for was the violently accelerating lunge that followed the jolt. Scott and a crewman crashed against a rear wall. McCoy and Christine Chapel were sent reeling back through two sections of Sickbay. In the bridge an African plant nurtured by Uhura flew through the air to smash against the elevator door. People were hurled bodily over the backs of their chairs. There was another fierce lurch of acceleration. The ship tossed like a rearing horse. Metal screamed. Lights faded. Finally, the *Enterprise* steadied.

From the floor where he'd been tumbled, Kirk looked at the screen.

Failure. The starless black still possessed it.

Weary, bruised, Kirk hauled himself back into his chair. The question had to be asked. He asked it. "Mr. Scott, are we still losing power?"

"Aye, sir. All we did was to pull away a bit. The best we can do now is maintain thrust against the pull to hold our distance."

"How long do we have?"

"At this rate of drain plus the draw on all systems—two hours, Captain."

As Kirk got to his feet, another wave of weakness swept over him. It passed—and he moved over to the computer station. "We're trying to hold our distance, Mr. Spock. Have you yet ascertained what we are holding the distance *from?*"

Spock, his eyes on his own screen, said, "I have not found out what that thing is, Captain. But it seems to have found us."

Kirk wheeled to the bridge viewer. In the center of its blackness a bright object had become visible—bright, pulsating, elongated.

Staring at it, Kirk said, "Mr. Chekov, prepare to launch a probe."

Bent to his hooded computer, Spock said, "Very confused readings, Captain—but that object is definitely the source of the energy drains."

"Mr. Chekov, launch probe," Kirk said.

"Probe launched, sir. Impact in seven point three seconds."

Without order Sulu began the countdown. "Six, five . . . four . . . three . . . two . . . one . . . *now!*"

The ship trembled. Lights blinked. But that was all.

"Mr. Chekov, do we still have contact with the probe?"

"Yes, sir. Data being relayed to Mr. Spock."

"Mr. Spock?"

The Vulcan's head was hidden under the computer's mound. "Readings coming in now, Captain. Length, approximately eleven thousand miles. Varying in width from two thousand to three thousand miles. Outer layer strewn with space debris and other wastes. Interior consists of protoplasm varying from a firmer gelatinous layer to a semi-fluid central mass."

He withdrew his head from the computer. "Condition . . . living."

The faces around Kirk were stunned. He looked away from them and back at Spock. "Living," he said. Then, his voice very quiet, he said, "Magnification four, Mr. Sulu. On the main screen."

He had expected a horror—and he received it. The screen held what might be a nightmare of some child who had played with a lab microscope—a monstrous, amoebalike protozoan. The gigantic nucleus throbbed, its chromosome bodies vaguely shadowed under its gelatinous, spotted skin. In open loathing, Kirk shut his eyes. But he could not dispel his searing memory of what continued to show on the screen.

In Sickbay's lab, McCoy was parading a pictured series of one-celled creatures. On the small viewscreen a paramecium, its cilia wriggling, came and went. Then McCoy said, "This is an amoeba."

If life was movement, ingestion, the thing was alive, a microscopic inhabitant of stagnant pools. As Kirk watched, a pseudopod extended itself, groping but intent on a fragment of food. There was a blind greed in the creature that sickened Kirk.

"I've seen them before," he said. "Like that, enlarged by microscope. But this thing out there is eleven thousand miles long! Are you saying that anything so huge is a single-celled animal?"

"For lack of a better term, Jim. Huge as it is, it is a very simple form of life. And it can perform all the functions necessary to qualify it as a living organism. It can reproduce, receive sense impressions, act on

170

them, and eat, though what its diet is I wouldn't know."

"Energy," Spock said. "Energy drained from us. I would speculate that this unknown life form is invading the galaxy like an infection."

"Mr. Spock, the *Intrepid* died of this particular infection. Why have we survived so long?"

"The *Intrepid* must have come upon it when it was hungry, low in energy. We are not safe, Captain. We merely have a little more time than the *Intrepid* had."

"Bones, this zone of darkness. Does the thing generate it itself as some form of protection?"

"That's one of the things we have to find out, Jim. We need a closer look at it."

"The closer to it we get, the faster it eats our energy. We're barely staying alive at this distance from it."

McCoy shut off his screen. "We could risk the shuttlecraft. With special shielding, it might—"

"I'm not sending anybody anywhere near that thing! Unmanned probes will give us the information we need to destroy it."

"I must differ with you, Captain," Spock said. "We have sent probes into it. They have told us some facts but not those we need to know. We're in no position to expend the power to take blind shots at it. We need a target."

McCoy said, "One man could go in . . . pinpoint its vulnerable spots."

"And the odds against his coming back?" Kirk cried. "How can I order anyone to take such a chance?"

"Who mentioned orders?" McCoy demanded. "You've got yourself a volunteer, Jim, my boy. I've already done the preliminary work."

"Bones, it's a suicide mission!"

"Doctor, this thing has reflexes. The unmanned probe stung it when it entered. The lurch we felt was the turbulence of its reaction."

"All right, Spock," McCoy said. "Then I'll have the sense to go slow when I penetrate it."

Spock studied him. "There is a latent martyr in you, Doctor. It is an affliction that disqualifies you to undertake the mission."

"Martyr?" McCoy yelled. "You think I intend to bypass the chance to get into the greatest living laboratory ever?"

"The *Intrepid* carried physicians and psychologists, Doctor. They died."

"Just because Vulcans failed doesn't mean a human will."

Kirk hit the table with his fist. "Will you both kindly shut up? I've told you! I'm not taking volunteers!"

"You don't think you're going, do you?" McCoy shouted.

"I am a command pilot!" Kirk said. "And as such, I am the qualified person. So let's have an end of this!"

"You have just *disqualified* yourself, Captain," Spock said. "As the command pilot you are indispensable. Nor are you the scientific specialist which I am."

McCoy glared at Spock. "Jim, that organism contains chemical processes we've never seen before and may never, let's hope, see again. We could learn more in one day than—"

"We don't have a day," Kirk said. "We have precisely one hour and thirty-five minutes. Then all our power is exhausted."

"Jim . . ."

"Captain . . ."

Kirk whirled on them both. "*I* will decide who can best serve the success of this mission! When I have made my command decision—command decision, gentlemen—you will be notified."

He turned on his heel and left them.

The solitude of his quarters felt good. He closed the door behind him, unhooked his belt and with his back turned to the clock's face deliberately stretched himself out on his bunk. Relax. Let the quiet move up, inch by inch, from his feet to his throbbing head. *Let go.* If you could just let go, answers sometimes welled up from an untapped wisdom that resisted pushing. "God, let me relax," Kirk prayed.

It was true. He *was* indispensable. There was no room in command authority for the heroics of phony modesty. As to Bones, he *did* have the medical-biological advantages he'd claimed. But Spock, the born athlete, the physical-fitness fanatic, the Vulcan logician and Science Officer, was both physically and emotionally better suited to withstand the stresses of such a mission. Yet who could know what invaluable discoveries Bones might make if he got his chance to make them? So it was up to him—Kirk. The choice was his. One of his friends had to be condemned to probable death. Which one?

He drew a long shuddering breath. Then he reached out to the intercom over his head and shoved its button. "This is the Captain speaking. Dr. McCoy and Mr. Spock report to my quarters at once. Kirk out."

The beep came as he sat up. "Engineering to Captain Kirk."

"Go ahead, Scotty."

"You wanted to be kept informed of the power drain, sir. All levels have sunk to fifty percent. Still draining. We can maintain power for another hour and fifteen minutes."

"Right, Scotty." He drew a hand over the bunk's coverlet, stared at the hand, and said, "Prepare the shuttlecraft for launching."

"What's that, sir?"

"You heard me, Scotty, Dr. McCoy will tell you what special equipment to install. Kirk out."

Of course. The knock on his door. He got up and opened it. They were both standing there, their mutual antagonism weaving back and forth between them. "Come in, gentlemen." There was no point, no time for suspense. "I'm sorry, Mr. Spock," Kirk said heavily.

McCoy flashed a look of triumph at Spock. "Well, done, Jim," he said. "I'll get the last few things I need and—"

Kirk stopped him in midstride. "Not you, Bones." He

turned to Spock. "I'm sorry, Spock. I am sorry you are the best qualified to go."

Spock nodded briefly. He didn't speak as he passed the crushed McCoy.

The door to the hangar-deck elevator slid open. Spock moved aside to allow McCoy to precede him out of it. "Do not suffer so, Doctor. Professional credentials are very valuable. But superior resistance to strain has occasionally proved more valuable."

"Nothing has been proven yet!" McCoy controlled himself with an effort. "My DNA code analyzer will give you the fundamental structure of the organism. You'll need readings on three light wavelengths from the enzyme recorder."

"I am familiar with the equipment, Doctor. Time is passing. The shuttlecraft is ready."

"You just won't let me share in this at all, will you, Spock?"

"This is not a competition, Doctor. Kindly grant me my own kind of dignity."

"Vulcan dignity? How can I grant you what I don't understand?"

"Then employ one of your human superstitions. Wish me luck, Dr. McCoy."

McCoy gave him a startled look. Without rejoinder, he shoved the button that opened the hangar-deck door. Beyond them the metallic skin of the chosen shuttlecraft gleamed dimly. Two technicians busied themselves with it, making some final arrangements. Spock, without looking back, walked through the hangar door. McCoy saw him climb into the craft. Then the door slid closed; McCoy, alone, muttered, "Good luck, Spock, damn you."

Kirk, on the bridge, waited. Then Sulu turned. "All systems clear for shuttlecraft launch, sir."

It was time to say the words. "Launch shuttlecraft."

The light winked on Sulu's console. Spock was on his way. Alone. In space, alone. Committed—given over to what he, his Captain, had given him over to. Kirk heard the elevator whoosh open. McCoy came

174

out of it. Kirk didn't turn. He said, "Lieutenant Uhura, channel telemetry directly to Mr. Chekov at the computer station."

The bridge speaker spoke. "Shuttlecraft to *Enterprise*."

"Report, Mr. Spock."

"The power drain is enormous and growing worse." Static crackled. "I am diverting all secondary power systems to the shields. I will continue communications as long as there is power to transmit."

Spock would be huddled now, Kirk knew, over the craft's control panel. He'd be busy shutting off power systems. Somehow Scott had suddenly materialized beside his command chair. "Captain! He won't have power enough to get back if he diverts it to his shields!"

"Spock," Kirk began.

"I heard, Captain. We recognized that probability earlier. But you will need information communicated."

"When do you estimate penetration?"

"In one point three minutes. Brace yourselves. The area of penetration will no doubt be sensitive."

What was Spock's screen showing? What was his closeup like? The details of the debris-mottled membrane, the enlarging granular structure of the protoplasm under it, two thousand miles thick?

"Contact in six seconds," Spock's voice said.

A tremor shook the *Enterprise*. That meant the massive shock of impact for the shuttlecraft. Its lights would dim, alone in the dimness inside the thing. Kirk seized the microphone.

"Report, Mr. Spock."

Silence reported. Had Spock already lost consciousness? The organism would try to dislodge the craft. It would convulse, its convulsions sending its painful intruder into a spinning vortex of repeated shocks.

"Spock . . ."

The voice came, weak now. "I am undamaged, Captain . . . relay to Mr. Scott . . . I had three percent power reserve . . . before the shields stabilized. I . . . will proceed with my tests . . . The voice faded . . .

then it returned. "Dr. McCoy . . . you would not . . . have survived this . . ."

Kirk saw that McCoy's eyes were moist. "You wanna bet, Spock?" His voice broke on the name.

"I am . . . moving very slowly now—establishing course toward . . . the nucleus."

Chekov, white-faced, called from the computer. "Sir, Mr. Spock has reduced his life support systems to bare minimum. I suppose to maintain communications."

Kirk's hand was wet on his microphone. "Spock, save your power for the shields."

Static sputtered from the microphone. Between its cracklings, words could be heard. "My . . . calculations indicate—shields . . . only forty-seven minutes." More obliterating static. It quieted. "Identified . . . Chromosome structure. Changes in it . . . reproduction process about to begin."

Ashen, McCoy cried, "Then there'll be *two* of these things!"

"Spock . . ."

Kirk got an earful of static. He waited. "I . . . am having . . . some difficulty . . . ship control."

Kirk looked away from the pain in McCoy's face. He waited again. As though it were warning of its waning usefulness, the mike spoke in jagged phrases. ". . . losing voice contact . . . transmitting . . . here are internal coordinates . . . chromosome bodies . . ."

Uhura turned from her console. "Contact lost, sir. But I got the coordinates."

"Captain!" It was Chekov. "The shuttlecraft shields are breaking! Fluctuations of energy inside the organism."

"Aye," Scott said. "It's time he got out of there."

There was nobody to look at but himself, Kirk thought. He was the man who had sent his best friend to death. He had sent Spock out to suffocate in the foul entrails of a primordial freak. That was a truth to somehow be lived with for the rest of his life. His chair lurched under him. The ship gave a shudder. Numbly, Kirk righted himself. Then, suddenly, in a blast of realization, he knew. "Bones!" The word tore from him in a shout. "He's alive! He's still alive! He made the craft kick the thing to force it to squirm —and let us know!"

Uhura spoke. "Captain, I'm getting telemetry."

"Mr. Chekov—telemetry analysis as it comes in."

McCoy was still brooding on what reproduction of the organism meant. "According to Spock's telemetry analysis, there are forty chromosomes in that nucleus ready to divide." He paused. "If the energy of this thing merely doubles, everybody and everything within a light year of it will be dead." He paced the length of the bridge and came back. "Soon there will be two of it, four, eight, and more— a promise of a combined anti-life force that could encompass the entire galaxy."

"That's what Spock knows, Bones. He knows. He knows we have no choice but to try and destroy it when he transmitted those coordinates of the chromosomes."

Scott said, "Look at your panel, Captain. The pull from the thing is increasing. The drain on our shields is getting critical."

"How much time, Scotty?"

"Not more than an hour now, sir."

"Shield power is an unconditional priority. Put all secondary systems on standby."

"Aye, sir."

"Bones, can we kill that thing without killing Spock? And ourselves, too?"

"I don't know. It's a living cell. If we had an antibiotic that—"

"How many billions of kiloliters would it take?"

"Okay, Jim. Okay."

Uhura, her face radiant, turned from her console. "I'm receiving a message from Mr. Spock, sir. Low energy channel, faint but readable."

"Give it to me, Lieutenant."

"Faint" wasn't the word. Weak was. Very weak now. Spock said, "I . . . am losing life support . . . and minimal shield energy. The organism's nervous energy is . . . only maximal within protective membrane . . . interior . . . relatively insensitive . . . sufficient charge of . . . could destroy . . . tell Dr. McCoy . . . he should have wished . . . me luck . . ."

The bridge people sensed the burden of the message. Silence fell, speech faltering at the realization that Spock was lost. Only the lowered hum of power-drained machinery made itself heard.

Kirk lay unmoving on the couch in his quarters. Spock was dead. And to what point? If he'd been able to transmit his information on how to destroy the thing, he would have died for a purpose. But even that small joy had been denied to him. Spock was dead for no purpose at all, to no end that mattered to him.

Without knocking, McCoy came in and sat down on the couch beside the motionless Kirk.

"What's on your mind, Dr. McCoy?"

"Spock," McCoy said. "Call me sentimental. I've been called worse things. I believe he's still alive out there in that mess of protoplasm."

"He knew the odds when he went out. He knew so much. Now he's dead." Kirk lifted an arm into the air, contemplating the living hand at the end of it. "What *is* this thing? Not intelligent. At least, not yet."

"It is disease," McCoy said.

"This cell—this germ extending its filthy life for eleven thousand miles—one single cell of it. When it's grown to billions, we will be the germs. We shall be the disease invading its body."

"That's a morbid thought, Jim. Its whole horror lies in its size."

"Yes. And when our form of life was born, what micro-universe did we destroy? How does a body destroy an infection, Bones?"

"By forming anti-bodies."

"Then that's what we've got to be—an anti-body." He looked at McCoy. Then, repeating the word "anti-body," he jumped to his feet and struck the intercom button. "Scotty, suppose you diverted all remaining power to the shields? Suppose you gave it all to them —and just kept impulse power in reserve?"

"Cut off the engine thrust?" Scott cried. "Why, we'd be sucked into that thing as helplessly as if it were a wind tunnell"

"Exactly, Mr. Scott. Prepare to divert power on my signal. Kirk out."

He turned to find himself facing McCoy's diagnostic Feinberger. "Got something to say, Bones?"

"Technically, no. Medically, yes. Between the strain and the stimulants, your edges are worn smooth. You're to keep off your feet for a while."

"I don't have a while. None of us do. Let's go . . ."

He took time to compose his face before he stepped out of the bridge elevator. He took his place in his command chair before he spoke into the intercom. "All hands, this is the Captain speaking. We are going to enter the body of this organism. Damage-control parties stand by—all decks secure for collision. Kirk out."

"It's now or never," he thought—and called Engineering.

"Ready, Mr. Scott?"

"Yes, sir."

"*Now*," Kirk said.

The ship took a violent forward plunge. Kirk, gripping his chair, glanced at the screen. The blackness grew denser as they sped toward it. "Impact— twenty-five seconds, sir," Sulu said intensely.

Then shock knocked Sulu from his chair. Something flared from the screen. Chekov, sprawled on the deck, looked up at his console as the ship steadied. "We're through, sir!" he shouted.

Uhura, recovering her position, called, "Damage parties report minimal hurt, Captain."

Kirk didn't acknowledge the information. The blackness on the screen had gone opaque. The *Enterprise*, lost in the vast interior of the organism, moved sluggishly through the lightlessness of gray jelly.

Engineering again. "Mr. Scott, we still have our impulse power?"

"I saved all I could, sir. I don't know if there's enough to get us out of this again. Or time enough to do it in."

"We have committed ourselves, Mr. Scott."

"Aye. But what are we committed to? We've got no power for the phasers."

McCoy made an impatient gesture. "We couldn't use them if we did. Their heat would rebound from this muck and roast us alive."

"The organism would love the phasers. It eats power—" Kirk broke off. A frantic Scott, rushing from the elevator, had caught his last word. "Power!" he cried. "That's the problem, Captain! If we can't use power to destroy this beast, what is it we *can* use?"

"Anti-power," Kirk said.

"What?" McCoy said.

Scott was staring at him. "This thing has a negative energy charge. Everything that has worked has worked in reverse. In its body, we're an anti-body, Scotty. So we'll use anti-power—anti-matter—to kill it."

Scott's tension relaxed like a pricked balloon. "Aye, sir! That it couldn't swallow! What good God gave you that idea, Captain?"

"Mr. Spock," Kirk said. "It's what he was trying to tell us before . . . we lost him. Mr. Chekov, prepare a probe. Scotty, we'll need a magnetic bottle for the charge. How soon?"

"It's on its way, laddie!"

"Mr. Chekov, timing detonator on the probe. We'll work out the setting. Mr. Sulu, what's our estimated arrival at the nucleus?"

"Seven minutes, sir."

"Jim, how close are you going to it?"

"Point-blank range. Implant it—and back away."

"But the probe has a range of—"

Kirk interrupted McCoy. "The eddies and currents in the protoplasm could drift the probe thousands of kilometers away from the nucleus. No, we must be directly on target. We won't get a second chance."

Kirk rubbed the stiffening muscles at the nape of his neck. "Time for another stimulant, Bones."

"You'll blow up. How long do you think you can go on taking that stuff?"

"Just hold me together for another seven minutes."

He took one of the minutes to address his Captain's log. "Should we fail in this mission, I wish to record here that the following personnel receive special citations: Lieutenant Commander Leonard McCoy, Lieutenant Commander Montgomery Scott,—and my highest recommendation to Commander Spock, Science Officer, who has given his life in performance of his duty."

As he punched off the recorder, Scott, hurrying back to the command chair, paused to listen to Sulu say, "Target coordinates programmed, sir. Probe ready to launch."

"Mr. Sulu, program the fuse for a slight delay." He swung to Chekov. "All non-essential systems on standby. Communications, prepare for scanning. Conserve every bit of power. We've got to make it out of this membrane before the explosion. Make it work, Scotty. Pray it works."

"Aye, sir."

"Mr. Chekov, launch probe at zero acceleration. Forward thrust, one tenth second."

"Probe launched," Chekov said.

The moment finally passed. Then the ship bucked to the sound of straining metal. In the dimness made by the fading lights of the bridge, the air became sultry, suddenly heavy, oppressive. Kirk could feel the racing of his body's pulses. Then the air was breathable again; Chekov, turning, said, "Confirmed, sir. The probe is lodged in the nucleus . . . close to the chromosome bodies."

Kirk nodded. "Mr. Sulu, back out of here the way we came in. Let's not waste time. That was a nice straight line, Mr. Chekov."

Chekov flushed with pleasure. "Estimate we'll be out in six point thirty-nine minutes, sir." He glanced back at his panel, frowning. "Captain! Metallic substance outside the ship!"

"Spock?" McCoy said.

Chekov flicked on the screen. "Yes, sir. It's the shuttlecraft, lying there dead on its side."

In one bound Kirk was beside Uhura. "Lieutenant, give me Mr. Spock's voice channel! High gain!"

The microphone shook in his hand as he waited for her to test the wave length. "Ready, sir," she said.

He waited again to try and steady his voice. "Mr. Spock, do you read me? Spock, *come in!*" He whirled to Scott. "Mr. Scott, tractor beam!"

"Captain . . . we don't have the time to do it! We've got only a fifty-three percent escape margin!"

"Will you kindly take an order, Lieutenant Commander? Two tractor beams on that craft!"

Scott reddened. "Tractor beams on, sir."

"Glad to hear it!" Kirk said—and incredibly the mike in his hand was speaking. "I . . . recommend you . . . abandon this attempt, Captain. Do . . . not risk the ship further . . . on my account."

Wordless, Kirk handed the mike to McCoy. McCoy looked at him and he nodded. "Shut up, Spock!" McCoy yelled. You're being rescued!" He returned the mike to Kirk.

Spock said, "Thank you, Captain McCoy."

Weak as he was, Kirk thought, he'd find the strength to cock one sardonic eyebrow.

Weak—but alive. A knowledge better than McCoy's stimulants. "Time till explosion, Mr. Chekov?"

"Fifty-seven seconds, sir."

"You're maintaining tractor beam on the shuttlecraft, Mr. Scott?"

"Aye, sir." But the Scottish gloom of Kirk's favorite engineer was still unsubdued. "However, I can't guarantee it will hold when that warhead explodes." He glanced at his board. Despite the dourness of his expectations, he gave a startled jump. "The power levels show dead, sir."

Then the power levels and everything else ceased to matter. The ship whirled. A white-hot glare flashed through the bridge. McCoy was smashed to the deck. In the glare Kirk saw Chekov snatched from his chair to fall unconscious at the elevator door. Uhura's body, on the floor beside her console, rolled to the ship's rolling. Disinterestedly, Kirk realized that blood was pouring from a gash in his forehead. A handkerchief appeared in his hand—and Sulu crawled away from him back in the direction of his chair. He sat up and tied the handkerchief around his head. It's what you did in a tough tennis game to keep the sweat out of your eyes . . . a long time since he played tennis . . .

"Mr. Sulu," he said, "can you activate the view-screen?"

Stars. They had come back. The stars had come back.

A good crew. Chekov had limped back to his station. Not that he needed to say it. But it was good to hear, anyway. "The organism is destroyed, Captain. The explosion must have ruptured the membrane. It's thrown us clear."

The stars were back. So was the power.

Kirk laid his hand on Scott's shoulder. "And the shuttlecraft, Scotty?"

Spock's voice spoke from the bridge speaker. "Shuttlecraft to *Enterprise*. Request permission to come aboard."

Somebody put the mike in his hand. "You survived that volcano, Mr. Spock?"

"Obviously, Captain. And I have some very interesting data on the organism that I was unable to . . ."

McCoy, rubbing his bruised side, shouted, "Don't be so smart, Spock! You botched that acetylcholine test, don't forget!"

"Old Home Week," Kirk said. "Bring the shuttlecraft aboard, Mr. Scott. Mr. Chekov, lay in a course for Starbase Six. Warp factor five."

He untied the bloody handkerchief. "Thanks, Mr. Sulu. I'll personally see it to the laundry. Now I'm off to the hangar deck. Then Mr. Spock and I will be breaking out our mountaineering gear."

A SELECTED LIST OF SCIENCE FICTION
FOR YOUR READING PLEASURE